A Bride for Finn
The Proxy Brides Book 5

A Bride for Finn
The Proxy Brides Book #5

Linda Ellen

A Bride for Finn

The Proxy Brides Series, Book 5
Written by Linda Ellen

Copyright © 2018 by Linda Ellen
Trade Paperback Release: November 2018
Electronic Release: November 2018
http://lindaellenbooks.weebly.com/

All rights reserved. This book may not be reproduced, scanned, or distributed in any printed or electronic form without permission from the author. Please do not participate in or encourage piracy of copyrighted materials in violation of the author's rights. All characters and storylines are the property of the author and your support and respect is appreciated.

Names, characters and incidents depicted in this book are products of the author's imagination or are used fictitiously. Although this book is a work of fiction, real locales, streets, and places were used. Brands are used respectfully. Details regarding the cities of Louisville, Kentucky and Brownville, Nebraska, in 1875 were taken from websites, information learned in person, photographs, and other information found online, such as Facebook groups.

The following story contains themes of real life, but is suitable for all ages, as it contains no illicit sex or profanity.

Cover design by Virginia McKevitt
   http://www.virginiamckevitt.com
Editing by Venessa Vargas
Proofreading by Kathryn Lockwood
Formatting by Christine Sterling

REVIEWS

A proxy marriage, traveling to a new city, and a legendary outlaw—all woven into the mosaic tapestry that is one of Linda Ellen's richly written worlds! *A Bride for Finn* takes us from the gem city of Louisville to the rustic wonder that is Brownville, Nebraska. Charise and Finn's romance grows passionate with each word. Couple that with the antics of the townspeople, and the underlying mystery of a certain infamous character, this is absolutely a world you can get lost in.

You can't help but submerge yourself in this love story that requires a leap of faith and the courage to leave behind the only home and family you've ever known for an adventure that would be told for generations.

This intricately layered tale, of taverns turned into barbershops, a proxy husband and a traveling porcelain tub is truly a wonder to read.

~*Venessa Vargas, Editor and Author*

An incredible love story! Linda brings the characters to life with the first stroke of her pen and I couldn't help but feel compassion for Finn right from the start. A handsome man with a successful career, he yearned for someone to share his life with. He had been in love but she had only used him, stepping on his heart with no regrets. With no suitable options in the town he lived in, he chose to order a mail-order-bride. I could feel his heartache as he was again taken advantage of and found himself waiting at the train depot for a bride that would not arrive. Feeling the bitterness of betrayal, he was about to give up until his brother offers a solution. But just as soon as happiness seems to be in his grasp a stupid accident happened!

Left standing at the altar, Charise had her own share of heartache. Being a mail-order-bride seemed to be a perfect solution to get her out of town and away from unpleasant memories. Finn seemed like an answer to prayer, but the man getting off the train sure didn't look like the man described in his letters. Had she made a big mistake?

Although I love the story for the romance, it's so much more. Drama, heartache, jealousy, humor, surprises and even an outlaw contribute to this amazing tale. A must read for anyone who craves good, clean, love stories.

~*Judy Glenn, Beta Reader*

Linda has once again created a wonderful story in which a reader would love to get lost. She continues her creative streak with *A Bride for Finn*, the 5th book in the new *The Proxy Brides* series.

Linda writes in a way that allows the reader to step into the story and live alongside its characters. The plot is fresh and original, the characters are well developed and relatable, and the writing flows like a gentle stream, allowing the reader to float along and enjoy the journey. I found Finn and Charise's story quite unique, having never heard of the proxy bride concept before. I loved Finn and Charise's love story.

Too often Historical Romance books fall into the formulaic plotlines revolving around the main characters either having a misunderstanding and walking away from the relationship, only to come together in the end or enduring one calamity after another to the point of being laughable. I appreciate that Linda doesn't fall into that pitfall and instead, creates characters that stick together through the rough patches.

A Bride for Finn is fresh, lovable, and sure to be a hit.

~Liz Austin, Beta Reader, Poet, Blogger

Table of Contents

Chapter 1	1
Chapter 2	19
Chapter 3	35
Chapter 4	53
Chapter 5	73
Chapter 6	93
Chapter 7	111
Chapter 8	135
Chapter 9	157
Chapter 10	179
Author Notes	196
Acknowledgements	199
Upcoming Proxy Bride Books (2018 Series)	200
About the Author	201
Other works by Linda Ellen	202

Chapter 1

April 1875
Train depot, Brownville, Nebraska

Phineas "Finn" Maynard wiped moisture from his face as he stared down the empty tracks.

Gloomy day. Wouldn't you know it would start to rain, **and** *the train would be late today?* He muttered an off-color word with a frustrated huff. *Sending for a mail-order-bride is nerve-racking enough without this.*

Turning to inspect his reflection in the sparkling glass of one of the brand new depot's windows, he saw what he expected to see—his dark, wavy hair plastered flat to his head and the collar of his white shirt no longer crisp from the laundry. The foul weather wasn't helping his only suit look any better either.

Glancing down, Finn frowned at the drooping flowers gripped tightly in his left hand—the hastily picked bouquet of black-eyed Susans he had thought Miss Irma McIntire might like.

So much for my romantic gesture—might as well chuck these...I wonder where the heck the train is... he pondered as he turned to go back inside the shelter of the depot. After taking only three steps, however, his eyes widened as the train's whistle sounded from around the bend, north of town. His heart kicked into a gallop and he swallowed nervously and reached up to unconsciously tug at his collar, thinking he had tied the blasted string tie too tightly in his rush to be on time for the train.

Within a minute, a gleaming black and gold locomotive of the Midland Pacific line, followed by its coal tender, passenger car and caboose, chugged around the curve. Belching black smoke from its massive stack, its bright red pilot, or cowcatcher, forged ahead through the mist. Soon the engineer skillfully braked to a stop and Finn stood back against the brick wall of the depot as a loud hiss accompanied a cloud of steam.

The conductor announced their arrival at Brownville before hurrying out to place the portable steps on the wooden surface of the platform. Then he reached up to assist as travelers began stepping down from the lone passenger car.

Finn nodded greetings as he recognized town folks such as JW Furnas and his wife, Ella. Next, Attorney Rupert Brown and his family of six boys exited the car, as well as a few others whose names escaped him at the moment.

Suddenly the small area between the building and the train filled up with people and he craned his neck and dodged heads, trying to catch a glimpse of Irma. Had she told him what she would be wearing? He hadn't thought to remember, as he hadn't figured on there being a crowd welcoming the blasted train. True, the arrival of the train was still an exciting novelty in town, as the railroad had just finished building the depot and laying the tracks a month prior, but he wished folks would just get out of his way.

A few more passengers disembarked, rushing forward to greet those who had come to meet them, but no new faces emerged. How could that be? Digging in his pocket, he retrieved the telegram from Irma when she'd received the money he wired through Western Union for her to purchase train tickets. Double-checking, he gave a nod as he read again that she would be arriving April 14 on the nine o'clock train. Tugging on his watch chain, he pulled it free of its pocket and pushed the crown on the stem to open the cover. *9:21...* He snapped the lid closed again and stashed it away to protect it from the moisture. *Where is she? Did something happen? Maybe she missed getting on in Nevada City?*

Minutes ticked by as he stood there dumbfounded, staring at the end of the car with the hope that his mail-order-bride had just fallen asleep on the thirty-some-odd mile trip and would disembark soon. Debating whether or not to board the car himself to see if she was, indeed, asleep on one of the seats, he glanced to the right as the last of the passengers' luggage, as well as the freight, were offloaded. He rifled one hand back through his once-combed hair, leaving it disheveled.

Suddenly the whistle blew again, and the conductor hollered out the customary, "All aboard!"

Several people who had been visiting the pastor of the Baptist church in town came out of the depot and walked toward the now empty passenger car, nodding to Finn as they passed by.

Just as Finn was about to step forward and speak to the conductor standing next to the train's portable steps, he felt a tap on his arm. Turning, he came face to face with the concerned blue-eyed gaze of his friend Charlie Cooper, Brownville's telegraph operator and railroad ticket agent. The smaller man tugged on the visor of his uniform cap and gave an apologetic shrug.

"Finn...I hate to deliver news like this, but..." Charlie cleared his throat and mumbled what sounded like, "I'm sorry," and thrust a small folded piece of paper into Finn's hand before turning and beating a swift retreat back inside the station.

With a frown, Finn stashed the now soggy bouquet under one arm and opened the telegram, reading Charlie's neat printing.

To Phineas Maynard, Brownville, Nebraska

From Irma McIntire, Chicago, Illinois

Had to get to my husband in California STOP Used your money for tickets STOP Sorry for deception STOP Will pay you back STOP Irma

Finn blinked drops of accumulated mist from his lashes as he re-read the words, which were now beginning to run together as the rain picked up. *Her **husband**? She took my money and bought tickets to go to...her HUSBAND?*

Immediately, he saw himself *again* standing with a bouquet, only that time it was at the front door of Susie Jeffers' house as she laughingly told him he only had himself to blame. That everyone in town knew she was over the moon for Brian Allenby. She had merely been using Finn to make Brian jealous—and it had worked. He saw again Brian's flashing white grin as he and Susie laughed together at Finn's expense while he turned and stumbled down the steps, their laughter echoing in his head with each step he trudged.

The hand holding the offending piece of paper curled into a hard fist as he realized that once again, he had trusted a female and she had made a big fool out of him.

Women! Are there any good ones out there?

Uttering a curse, Finn cast the ruined flowers and

crumpled telegram to the ground. Turning on his heel, he stomped home grousing and muttering as the heavens opened and the rain began to pour down.

No woman will ever do this to me again. Never again!

"So, you just gonna give up on gettin' married, then?" Finn's brother, Samuel, asked with a teasing grin.

Standing side by side, one would not think they were even brothers, as Sam had inherited their father's burley physique, light brown, wavy hair, and brown eyes, while Finn had taken after their mother's side of the family—dark brown hair and dark blue eyes. Sam wore a full beard and mustache and favored wearing brown plaid shirts with suspenders, while Finn kept clean-shaven and tended to wear soft cotton shirts with a vest. Also, Sam stood four inches taller and outweighed him by at least seventy-five pounds.

Finn sent him a glare and opened his mouth to answer, but his brother chuckled as he sent yet another log through the sawmill's blade, thereby causing Finn to have to wait until the noise ceased.

Oh, the screech of that blade. Finn had hated the sound of it cutting through the wood ever since Sam had exchanged the mill's original overshot water wheel with a turbine and replaced the original up and down, or sash-type saw with a circular saw.

The sash saw—a thin, straight blade held in a wooden sash frame that cut only on the down stroke—had been installed by their father when he built the mill and it had been fine in Finn's opinion. But Sam, fresh out of the military at the end of the war, had seen more industrialized cities and felt the need to modernize and increase the mill's speed and power. He was sure Brownville would be a thriving river town in the next decade or two and he wanted to be prepared for the building boom he was sure would come.

Finn had argued against the change, insisting that the frustration of the noise and the greater potential for accidents outweighed the additional product that could be produced per hour. Sam told him he was crazy.

Now as the squealing of the blade against the wood made him grit his teeth, but not wishing to hear the customary ribbing from his brother, Finn resisted the urge to stuff his fingers in his ears as the saw made short work of the log.

"I don't know," he grumbled when the din abated, picking up a few wood chips and tossing them aside with a huff of aggravation. "Danged if I'm not tired of closing the shop at night and plodding up the steps to eat alone. But you know as well as I that the only single females in town are either way too young or way too old—other than Bertha Simmons, who's got to be a good eight inches taller than me, and the laundress, Elvira Davis, who talks a nonstop blue streak and never lets a body get a word in edgewise." He shook his head as he thought of times he had been shanghaied by her on the street, unable to get away. *I ain't that desperate for company... least wise yet.* "And you know I'm not one for seeking out female companionship at the Lucky Buck," he added with a pointed look at his older brother, whom he knew had ventured into the aforementioned saloon for that reason at least a time or two.

Samuel chuckled at that last remark, unconsciously smoothing one hand over his bushy beard. "Ma's not here anymore to skin us alive for patronizing the Lucky, like she threatened a hundred times." He cringed slightly under Finn's accusing glare before continuing, "But still, there's gotta be some way for a fella to find a wife around here—not that I'm in the market, mind you," he added quickly. "Ma would tell you to pray about it...but I'm guessin' you've done that too, right?"

Finn gave a half-hearted shrug. He *had* prayed about it...sort of. Hadn't he?

Both men lapsed into silence as Sam sent another log through the saw. Finn leaned against a support beam, crossed his feet at his ankles, and shoved his hands deep into his trouser pockets as he stared at the sawdust-covered floor, discouraged and disheartened.

Pushing the split, rough boards aside once they cleared the sharp, metal teeth, Sam looked over at his younger brother. "Hey," he snapped his fingers, getting Finn's attention. "Instead of having a mail-order-bride travel *here* to get married—why don't you hop the train and go to *her*? That way, you can also see what she looks like and all and decide before you tie the knot. Then bring her back with you on the train already legal and proper-like. You could even spend your weddin' night in a hotel or somethin'," he added with a wiggle of his bushy brows.

For the first time in days, Finn's lips curved into a spontaneous smile and his dark blue eyes twinkled like the midnight sky. "Now why didn't *I* think of that? Brother of mine, that's the best idea you've come up with in a month of Sundays!"

Sam just smiled and gave a nod. "I have my moments," he agreed, "and hey, if this thing works for *you*, I just might try it myself!"

This prompted the brothers to let go a few chuckles in easy camaraderie as Sam sent one of the rough boards back through for another pass to knock the remaining bark off the side.

Finn left his brother to his work, deciding to head on over to the telegraph office right then to put a new ad in some of the eastern newspapers' romance columns.

He laughed to himself when he realized there was a definite spring in his step.

Two weeks later in Louisville, Kentucky

Charise Willoughby let herself in the door of the two-room apartment she shared with her friend, Beth Ann Gilmore, and slammed it behind her, startling her redheaded roommate as she stood at their tiny stove stirring what looked like a pot of potato soup. Beth Ann jumped and turned her head, her mouth open and her green eyes wide.

"What in blue blazes..." she paused, perusing her friend's face. "Uh oh...don't tell me. You saw *him* again," It was a statement, not a question. Beth Ann knew her friend of five years never got that angry unless Ethan Breckinridge II was involved.

Charise flung her reticule onto the chair near the door and began unbuttoning the jacket of her favorite light blue, linen outfit, which had fancy embroidery decorating the snug bodice and waist, and a short, form-fitting jacket. She had worked many weeks on the finishing touches. A small, feathered hat matched the ensemble and contrasted richly with her dark sable hair. Tossing the jacket onto the chair, she ripped the hat off and hurled it onto the pile while she tried to get her adrenaline under control from the oh-so-recent encounter.

Her face was red with anger and tendrils of her long, mahogany hair had worked loose from its thick braid hanging in its customary place over her left collarbone. Flicking a look in her roommate's direction, she crossed her arms over her middle and blew out an irritated breath, reliving the agonizing humiliation of seeing her ex-fiancé with his new *wife*. "Yes...along with *her*, of course!"

Beth Ann put down the ladle she was using and turned fully toward her friend. "Don't let it bother you, Char, honey," she tried to soothe, using the shortened version of Charise's name as she always did, pronouncing it like *Shar*. "Despite the fact that his father is rich old Ethan Breckinridge of Breckinridge, Collier and Prentice, Attorneys at Law—or maybe *because* of that—he's a loser, not to mention a low-down skunk."

"I can't *help* but be bothered, Beth! To think I almost *married* that...that slimy *toad!* But every time I remember standing in the bride's room at the church, adjusting my veil, and having Mrs. D'Agostino knock on the door and tell me Ethan sent word that he was calling off the wedding—at the absolute *last* minute—I just want to crawl into a hole and pull the dirt in on top of me!"

Charise jammed fisted hands onto her hips as she continued, "And now, to see him with that *Celeste* creature, strolling toward me on the street all lovey-dovey, practically looking through me as if I weren't even there...it makes me want to chew up and spit nails!"

Growling in frustration and grinding her teeth for a moment as if doing that very thing, she finally made herself consciously draw in a deep breath, hold it, and then let it out slowly, shaking her hands for good measure, as if shaking off the *mad*. It was a method her mother had taught her many years ago and it never failed to make her feel at least a bit better. Glancing back at her friend again, she managed an impish smile. "Today, I nearly leapt at them to scratch their eyes out...only I couldn't decide who to aim at first, him or her."

The longtime friends chuckled together at that and Charise wandered over toward the kitchen corner of their miniscule apartment as Beth Ann turned back to the stove and began dipping her delicious potato soup into bowls.

"Well, come on honey, let's eat supper. I managed to get some cornbread in the oven as soon as I got home, and it should be about done." Opening the oven door, she grinned and nodded. "Yep, nice and golden brown." Grabbing a potholder, she pulled the pan out of the hot interior and placed it onto the scarred wooden surface of their two-seater table.

"Grab the butter, will ya, hon?"

Working together, they soon had supper on the table and were enjoying their evening meal.

After discussing a few innocuous subjects, Charise

glanced at her friend in between bites and admitted, "Bethie, I just don't know what I'm going to do, but I do know *one* thing...I can't keep going on like this. It's been six months since he jilted me, and every time I start to feel like I'm getting over it and making headway, WHAM, I see him again and it starts all over. I wish..." she paused, mulling over the words. "I wish I could just move somewhere else. But...I don't have any money saved up and I wouldn't have a clue how to move to a new town, find a job and a place to live, find new friends, a church, a new *life*—" she paused, a shudder of dread coursing through her body.

"What you need is a husband," Beth Ann stated flatly, taking a big bite of cornbread.

"A *husband?*" Charise expelled a rather unladylike snort. *Fat chance.* "No man has even asked me out to dinner since it happened—you'd think I've been branded as a scarlet woman or something. There are no prospects of gaining a husband, even on the distant horizon, my friend." A smidgen of jealousy made her add, "You don't have to worry about things like that, since you've got your Stanley."

Beth Ann rolled her eyes at the mention of her long-time boyfriend, predictable, dependable...*boring* Stanley.

The redhead gave Charise the eye and waved her spoon at her. "Listen honey, you're a beautiful, smart, kind girl. Any man should be proud as punch to have you for a wife.

What you need is a whole pot of men to choose from," she added with a wickedly playful spark in her eye as she dipped her spoon back into her bowl and scooped out a big chunk of potato.

Charise looked at her as if she'd lost her mind and began liberally spreading butter on another piece of cornbread. "And just *where*, might I ask, does one find a whole *pot* of men for the choosing?"

Beth Ann swallowed her spoonful of soup and washed it down with a drink of tea before fixing her eyes on Charise. "In the newspaper."

"The *newspaper?*" Charise's eyebrows scrunched, and then her eyes opened wide in shock. "You mean...you're not talking about *mail-order-brides,* are you?"

Beth Ann couldn't hold back the grin any longer and it burst forth on her face. "Well—why not? Lots of girls have found their men that way. And from what I've read, the marriages usually turn out pretty well."

"Usually is a very important word in that sentence, my friend. My luck, I'd be the exception to the rule!"

Beth Ann merely shrugged, as if she knew something Charise did not. "Well, it wouldn't hurt to take a look-see, would it?"

Before Charise could answer, her friend wiped her

mouth on a napkin and hopped up from her chair, quickly retrieving what appeared to be several newspapers already opened and folded back at the matrimonial sections.

Charise's eyes widened as she took in the sight. She had known the *Courier-Journal* boasted a matrimonial column as she had heard it spoken of in passing, but she had never actually read any of the ads. Reaching for the stack, she saw they were the Louisville paper, as well as the *Cincinnati Enquirer*, the *Chicago Tribune*, and even the *Boston Globe*!

"Where in the world did you get all these?"

Beth Ann let out a mischievous giggle. "Old Mr. Hinkle across the hall. He has subscriptions and gets them every week. He let me have these after he'd finished with them."

"You didn't tell him *why* you wanted them, did you?" Charise gasped. Her friend just laughed.

"You worry too much, Char. Come on, let's finish up and have a look, huh?"

So, the girls quickly cleared their places, cleaned the dishes, and then sat down at the little table to see if they could find the proverbial *pot of men.*

They had been pouring over the ads for an hour, laughing at some, and shaking their heads at others. Some were too young, while others were old enough to be Charise's father.

Several were widowers with a whole passel of children. One said he lived in Indian territory and his prospective wife would need to already know how to ride and shoot like a man, as he wouldn't have time to teach her. A few came right out and plainly said they wanted what amounted to a housekeeper, but most seemed like honest, upright men looking to find the love of their lives—or at least a pleasant wife with which to spend the rest of their days.

The girls had cut out the best sounding prospects and laid them aside for Charise to answer.

From the *Boston Globe*, Beth Ann read aloud, *"33-year-old man seeking woman for matrimony. She must be of good moral character, Christian preferred, age 21-35, not too tall or short, pleasant looking, and able to read and write. I am of medium height, have a trim build, with dark hair and dark blue eyes. Teeth are decent. I can provide a comfortable home. I live a clean, sober life and would make the right lady a good, faithful husband. Please reply with details about yourself to Phineas Maynard, Brownville, Nebraska."*

"Hmm, that one sounds good..."

"Yes, he does..." Beth Ann agreed, raising an eyebrow at her friend. "I think you should write to this one right now and get it in the mail in the morning."

Feeling an urgency that her friend was right, Charise gave an agreeing nod, gathered paper, pen and ink, and set about writing her first mail-order-bride letter. The girls batted ideas back and forth as her elegant script slowly began to fill the page.

Dear Mr. Maynard,

I saw your advertisement in the newspaper today and thought I would write. To start off with, I am 25, a Born-Again Christian, am 5'4", with a decent figure, dark hair, and dark brown eyes, and blessed with straight teeth.

As you can see, I can write, and reading is one of my favorite pastimes, especially novels. I've never been married, although I was once engaged. I work as a seamstress and make my own clothing, and reside with a female friend in a small apartment. I can cook, and I love to clean. For personal reasons, I am looking to leave my hometown and start over, and was pleased to read that you lead a clean, sober life and pledge to be a faithful husband.

Since you are 33, may I ask if you've ever been married or have any children, since you didn't say specifically in your ad? As you requested a Christian, I'm assuming you are one as well, which is a relief, as that is also one of my requirements.

If you feel we might make a pleasant pair, please reply back to the address on the envelope.

Yours sincerely,

Charise Olivia Willoughby

Satisfied that she had said enough, but not too much, she blotted the ink dry, folded and inserted the pages in the carefully addressed envelope, and put the finished correspondence aside.

For good measure, she wrote a similar letter to each of the ads she and Beth had torn from the papers. Once mailed, Charise knew she would be on pins and needles to receive return missives.

She just hoped she didn't have to wait too long!

CHAPTER 2

*I*t had been two months of letter writing and decision making. Charise had answered four ads and all four men had written her back within the first two weeks...or at least she had received letters from them. The first letter, from a man somewhere in the wilds of Wyoming, stated that he could neither read nor write and he had come into town on his *once-a-year* visit and had the bartender write the letter for him. The bartender explained that the man, Eustis Haymaker, wanted a smart woman for a wife that knew how to do all of the things he didn't know. Charise politely passed on that one.

The second letter was from a man who confessed that he hadn't mentioned his five children in his ad because he was afraid he would get no responses, just like the other four times he had paid for ads. That, and the fact that he admitted he was 48 years old *and* declared he wanted a wife in name only, as he did NOT want any more children, caused Charise to pass him along as well. All prospect number three did was reply to Charise's questions with one or two word answers and mention that he wasn't much of a talker. Matter of fact—in his words—he was looking for a wife who enjoyed silent evenings by the fire when not a word would be spoken between them. In addition, he divulged that he lived a two-day trip by wagon from his nearest neighbor, which kind of put a damper on him. By that time, Charise was beginning to think Beth Ann's idea was one of her worst. *So much for her proverbial pot of men for me to choose from!*

And then, she received Finn's reply.

Charise immediately felt drawn to the way Mr. Maynard worded his missive, and she admired his neat, confident handwriting. His sense of humor had truly struck a chord with her, and she found answering his letters as easy as conversing with a friend.

Due to the length of time it took for letters to travel the nearly 650-mile distance between them, they had only exchanged three letters each, and so they had put their hearts into each one. Finn shared his faith and a bit about his family, and Charise replied along the same vein. He described his small town of only a little over two hundred residents and mentioned some of the more *unique* characters; Charise enjoyed those sections and even read some of it aloud to Beth Ann. He shared with her that he was the town barber, and his brother owned the sawmill. She talked about her job and her roommate and what life was like in Louisville—a large and fairly metropolitan city of over one hundred ten thousand inhabitants, nestled along the falls of the Ohio.

In his last letter, Finn had sent along a photograph. Although it was one taken years before, he assured her that he still looked much the same, just a bit older. From what she could see, he had a pleasant face and was a bit on the lanky side, but handsome in his own way. She found she liked his features.

He had proposed in that letter and declared that if she accepted his suit, he would make the trip to Louisville to meet and marry her, without the expectation of her traveling all the way to Nebraska unescorted—as prospective grooms of mail-order-brides generally did. She wrote back with her acceptance and appreciation for his care and thoughtfulness, and included a photograph of herself. It, too, was an older one, taken of her family the last time they had been together. Charise hadn't had the funds to have another portrait made since then. Although she was only fifteen in the picture, she assured him that she looked pretty much the same.

On this day, the fifth of June, she stood in the doorway of the apartment, holding a telegram from Finn, which informed her of the date and time that her future husband would be arriving to meet and wed her, should they both find one another amenable. He had picked the nineteenth of June, exactly two weeks hence. The last line stated he hoped he was giving her enough time, but he was anxious to get their future on its way.

Closing her eyes and pressing the folded missive to her heart, an excited shiver ran down the length of her body. *Two weeks! I have so much to do in that time...let's see, I have to finish my wedding dress and the veil...I want to put some finishing touches on my traveling outfit...I need to make sure all of my keepsakes are packed correctly in Mama's old steamer trunk so that none of them break on the long trip... Oh my goodness—two weeks! Two weeks from today, I'll become Mrs. Finn Maynard.*

Oh Lord...am I doing the right thing?

Finn walked out of the depot after sending the telegram to Charise...*Charise, I already love her name. I hope she's as elegant and ladylike as her moniker...*

He had received her last letter, in which she had graciously accepted his proposal, and sent a photograph of herself, her parents, and her two brothers, whom he knew from her second letter were now all deceased. Although still quite young in the portrait, he could tell even then she had the makings of a genteel lady—the way she held herself straight, her hands folded just so, her dainty chin tilted up, the hint of a smile as if she was thinking of a secret, and her eyes focused on the camera.

He liked what he saw there, very much. So much in fact that the image of her had spurred his determination to move forward with their union. A sense of possessiveness had unexpectedly seized him and he found he wanted to stake his claim on her before someone else snapped her up. *Most of the men in Louisville must be blind, stupid, or both to have missed out on such a prize as Miss Charise Willoughby.*

Ah well, as they say—their loss is my gain!

As he walked back to his barbershop, his steps light, he noted a few of his regulars had gathered outside the locked door and were waiting for him, so he quickened his pace. Unlocking the door amidst their grumbles about being kept waiting, he began preparations to shave old Cyrus Ames while they wandered inside. Charlie Grawemeyer and Cliff Fulton took their customary seats to wait their turns.

He noticed they were grinning at him like three cats about to pounce on a bowl of cream—three gray haired, gap-toothed, wrinkle-faced cats, that is.

Pausing in the act of snapping the cape free of hair from the last customer, Finn met each man's gleam. "What's got you three so amused this fine day?"

Charlie and Cliff exchanged looks and snickered together as Cyrus cackled before answering, "When's your lady love due to arrive from *Ken*-tuck-y, Finny boy?"

Musing about the fact that there were no secrets in a town this size, Finn sent him a scowl. Fluffing the cape around the old man, he purposely tied the neck a tad too tight, causing the end of the cackle to come out a might on the strangled side. "I told you, old man," he growled in mock anger, "stop calling me *Finny Boy*. I'm a grown man, not a wet behind the ears kid anymore."

Cyrus let out a snort. "Pshaw. Compared to me, sonny, you're still a pup—and it remains to be seen if you're still wet behind the ears or not." For good measure, he pointed a gnarled finger at Finn and spouted, "You respect your elders, you young whippersnapper!"

They all got a good chuckle out of that one, including Finn.

Some things never changed. Finn shook his head with a grin, knowing old Cyrus was just yanking his chain. He had known all three men since '54, when he had been just twelve years old and his family had joined a wagon train along with nine other wagons. Each were following after Richard Brown, the man who had built the first log cabin in a choice spot along the Missouri River in Nebraska and had called his new settlement *Brownville*. A younger—but still old in a youngster's eyes—Cyrus, had yelled at him and Sam as they chased one another in front of the old man's team of oxen.

Brown had predicted a rush of settlers would begin streaming into the area the following spring and come they did, either overland in wagons or floating down the river on flatboats. Cyrus had opened a gristmill, Finn's father had established a lumberyard and sawmill, and the port city had grown by leaps and bounds; so quickly that it had even been considered as a possible location for the territorial capital. A post office had been established the following year—albeit in a corner of the mercantile—with Cliff Fulton as the first postmaster.

Being in on the birth and establishment of a new town had been exciting times for the pioneers, including twelve-year-old Phineas Maynard. He still felt pride in what they had accomplished in such a short time.

Snapping back to the present, he realized the old-timers were staring at him with twinkling eyes, waiting for his answer. Finn set to work lathering up Cyrus' leathery cheeks as he had innumerable times before. Feeling the intense weight of their stares, he cleared his throat, knowing he might as well tell them his plans, or they would pester him until he did.

"To answer you buzzards, I just sent her a telegram letting her know that I'll be in Louisville in two weeks to meet her and marry her."

Cliff leaned forward and took his ever-present pipe out of his mouth. "You *did?* What'd she say to *that?*"

Finn began sharpening his razor on the strop hanging on the side of the chair and shrugged one shoulder. "She hasn't replied yet." Testing the edge with his thumb and finding it satisfactory, he turned to Cyrus and positioned his hands to commence his shave, but flicked a glance at the two old geezers leaning forward in their chairs and mentioned casually, "But she sent me a picture of her."

That set them to squawking like three old women. Finn couldn't help but chuckle as he warned Cyrus not to move if he didn't want to lose an ear, or maybe part of his nose.

"Is she a pretty filly?" Charlie asked, but before Finn could answer, the elder sat back in his chair, his old bones challenging the rickety piece of furniture on the amount of creaks and pops they could produce. Reaching into his shirt pocket for his ever-ready bag of tobacco, he began filling his corncob pipe, a familiar far away look in his eyes as he stared straight ahead. Finn knew before the oldster said a word that they were about to hear again the saga of his Cordelia.

"My Delia was sure a pretty little filly when we married. So young, so sweet and innocent—heck we were both..." he began the habitual reminiscence about the love of his life, now long passed on. Finn figured Charlie to be close to ninety by now, and pretty much all alone—his wife was gone, his sons and daughters old and the grandkids and great-grandkids were leading busy lives in larger, more exciting towns than Brownville, Nebraska. He knew for a fact the old man's family hardly ever wrote.

As he worked on Cyrus' chin and Charlie droned on,

Finn let his mind wander a bit to the past two months and the letters he had exchanged with his bride-to-be. He hadn't spent much time on the other answers he had received to the matrimonial ads he had placed in far away papers. They were women that had said upfront they had no time for *religion*, women who said they wanted a marriage in name only because they didn't want children, and one who said she was close to fifty, but had gone ahead and written him just in case he'd change his mind about wanting a younger woman. He'd started to think that maybe all of the good ones had been taken...

And then he'd received a letter from Charise.

In her elegant handwriting, she had told about herself, had answered every point in his ad, and had even asked him a few questions. There was just something different about her letter, and it wasn't just the subtle hint of roses emanating from the paper. For the life of him, he couldn't put his finger on it...but it was almost as if they already knew one another. He knew that was impossible, as she'd never been out of Louisville and he'd never ventured anywhere near it—even during the war. But reading her letter—it was as if her soul reached out and touched his. Like they were destined to meet—and to fall in love.

He let out a soft snicker as those last few thoughts went through his mind. The three old geezers sitting in his shop would really give him the business if he spoke those thoughts aloud. But *dad blast it*, it's how he felt! And with each subsequent letter Charise Willoughby had written him, he felt it more and more.

Danged if this idea of Sam's hadn't been right on the money. Finn somehow *knew* he had found his future. The only thing left to make sure of it was actually meeting her in person. That would be the deciding factor. If he was drawn to her physically...if *she* was attracted to *him*... *Then,* they could start their new life together.

He couldn't wait to receive her reply to his telegram!

The days passed quickly after Finn received his intended's reply: *Nineteenth is fine STOP Have given job and roommate notice STOP Will be ready and waiting STOP Charise*

Knowing it would take nearly five days by rail, considering all of the stops and the many times he would have to change trains between rail lines along the way east through Iowa, Illinois and Indiana before heading south to Kentucky, Finn set things in motion to leave early on Saturday, the fourteenth. His brother had assured him he would keep an eye on his shop while he was gone.

Friday evening, Finn headed over to the mill to bid Sam goodbye.

As he walked in, he saw Sam standing next to his new helper, sixteen-year-old Toby Keller, apparently giving the young man instructions. Finn heard the boy yell over the whir of the water-driven machinery, "Yes, sir!"

Turning, Sam spotted Finn approaching and he smiled in greeting as he reached over to flip the lever on the saw blade to disengage it from the turbine.

"All set to go get your lady?" Sam asked with a grin as he reached out to give his brother a friendly slap on the back.

"Yep. I'll catch the nine o'clock train in the morning and get to Louisville by noon on the nineteenth—that is, barring any train robberies, derailments, or bridge washouts," Finn joked.

Sam chuckled as he slipped his gloves off to swipe at the sweat on his forehead. "Well, let's hope none of those happen and you have a safe trip...and I hope Miss Charise didn't actually send a photograph of her roommate instead, but is everything you think she is," he added with a wink.

Refusing to allow any negative thoughts to enter his mind regarding his fiancée, Finn merely grunted in answer as he dug into one of his trouser pockets. "Here's the keys to the shop and the storage shed out back, although there shouldn't be any reason you'd have to get in there while I'm gone...but just in case," he explained with a shrug as he reached out and deposited them in his brother's outstretched palm.

Sam slipped them into his pocket with an answering nod. "I'll keep an eye out. But I don't expect anything will happen while you're gone...except for all the men in town becoming bewhiskered and shaggy."

Finn laughed and shook his head. "What can I say? I-."

"Oh no!" a voice shouted from high up over his left shoulder. Both men jerked their attention to the pile of rough logs to the left, just as the large one on top began rolling their way, having been dislodged in error by the clumsy adolescent.

"Look out!" Finn shouted as he made to pull Sam out of the way of the seven hundred pound log and jump clear of it himself—but in the melee, things went woefully wrong.

Pain knifed through Finn's leg just before his world went dark.

Fighting his way back to consciousness, Finn managed to pry his eyes open in response to his brother's urging, but immediately wished he hadn't, as a nearly unbearable strike of pain made itself known in the region of his right leg, and a lesser one—just barely—at the back of his head. He let out an agonized groan.

"Take it easy, brother," Sam cautioned as Finn shifted his body to try and escape the unknown cause of his torture. "I've sent Toby for Doc Reeves. Try not to move, Finny," he cautioned, resorting to the affectionate nickname he had used when they were boys. "Your leg's in a bad way."

"Wh...what happened?" Finn stammered and groaned, striving to remember and understand why he was now lying on the sawdust-covered floor of the mill with his right leg in excruciating misery.

"That stupid kid did the exact opposite of what I told him about making sure the pile of logs was secure for the night," Sam grumbled. "Because of him, the top log rolled off and gotcha."

"Oh..." Finn mumbled, gritting his teeth at the unbelievable pain. "Like you did that time and Pa almost kicked?" he managed to razz his brother concerning a near tragic happening when they were young themselves.

Sam snorted in agreement. "Yeah, something like that. Only Pa was able to jump out of the way and not get hurt."

"Mmmm don't remind me," Finn moaned.

Just then, they both heard a commotion near the door as Doc Reeves came hurrying in, followed by the hapless Toby.

"Move back a bit, Sam. Let's see what we have here," the doctor said and Finn, his eyes shut tight against the agony, felt his brother move out of the doc's way.

After a cursory inspection that caused Finn to yell out in pain before clamping his teeth, the doctor determined that they should get him over to his office as quickly and efficiently as they could, so that he could work on him under better conditions.

Finn barely heard their discussion before once again slipping into the blessed oblivion of unconsciousness.

The first thing he sensed as awareness slowly came back was that he was lying on something soft, rather than suffering the added annoyance of sawdust and woodchips digging into his back. Then, he had the sensation that his right leg seemed unusually heavy. He moved his hand downward to investigate.

"He's waking up, finally. Good. Good," the doctor's voice came from nearby.

Finn opened his eyes and blinked his sight into focus, seeing not only Doc Reeves, but Sam standing close.

"What happened?" he croaked, his voice rough.

The doctor lowered himself into a chair next to the bed and reached to gently turn Finn's head toward the light as he examined his eyes. "I'm afraid you hit your head rather hard on the floor as you were knocked down, causing some concussion...as well as suffering damage to your right leg—several fractures of the tibia," he explained as he checked out Finn's pupils. "The breaks were bad, but none came through the skin. I've set them and your leg is now encased in a sturdy cast. You should recover fully in a matter of weeks if you stay off of it and let it heal."

Finn shook his head and winced, trying to get up as the memory of his impending trip raked through his mind. "No...I've got to go to Louisville...Charise...she's waiting..." he bit out past the sharp stabbing pain his movements were causing his injured limb.

Sam's big hands suddenly clamped on his arms to hold him still as he warned in his most firm *big-brother* voice, "Little brother, listen to me—don't try to get up. You've got to stay still and let yourself heal. Besides, you've got a concussion—right Doc?"

"But Sam," Finn argued, raising his head and feeling the room starting to spin. Dropping back onto the pillow, he reached out and gripped the front of his brother's shirt. "I've got to get there. She's waiting for me. She's quit her job already...somebody else will scoop her up and take her from me...I've got to go..."

He felt Sam give his arms a squeeze. "Calm down, brother. I'll go get her and bring her here. Don't worry."

Finn couldn't seem to make sense of what was happening. Sam would go and get Charise?

"But...what if she won't come with you? She thinks we're getting married in Louisville. She's made plans..."

At this, Doc Reeves leaned over so that Finn could see him. He was smiling as if he had a secret. His next words shocked both of the Maynard brothers.

"Then Sam will marry her by proxy, and bring her back to you."

CHAPTER 3

Charise woke up early on the nineteenth and immediately experienced butterflies in the region of her stomach.

Today is my wedding day! Today, I'll meet Finn and become Mrs. Phineas Maynard.

Suppressing a girlish giggle, she sat up and swung her legs over the side of the bed and reached for Finn's last letter resting on her nightstand. She had received it just a few days before, and had read it numerous times—he was so sweet, assuring her that he believed God had brought them together and he couldn't wait to meet her in person. Shyly, he confessed that he hoped she would find his looks pleasant enough to want to view over the breakfast table every morning for the rest of their lives. In it, he had also told her that he would have a blue neckerchief—her favorite color—tied around his right arm to help her identify him on the crowded train platform. Then, he had ended the letter with, "Do you think you'll enjoy answering to *Mrs. Phineas Maynard* for the rest of your life?"

Mrs. Phineas Maynard...I can't wait!

She had finished two new outfits, a traveling ensemble to wear on most of the trip, and one to wear for Finn's first vision of her. The latter was an afternoon dress made of light blue silk, the hue of the summer sky, with royal blue piping that highlighted the square neckline, pointed bodice, ruffled three-quarter sleeves, and the hem, which just barely touched the ground. Although it sported a fashionable bustle, it was a modest one, and she'd chosen not to have the customary three-foot train at the back, as she abhorred the dirt they inevitably collected.

Finn's train would be pulling in to Central Station at Seventh and River Road at ten o'clock, and Beth Ann, angel of a friend that she was, had insisted she accompany Charise to the depot. It was, after all, a large, busy, confusing place. Their plan was for she and Finn to meet and if they found one another mutually acceptable, they would take a leisurely walk together to the Hotel Victoria, situated two blocks up and two blocks over from the station, allowing them to spend some time in its comfortable eatery getting to know one another.

Everything was ready. She'd given her notice at work and the ladies in the alterations department at Fessenden and Stewart had given her a small going away party—sandwiches, punch and cake—during their lunch hour. That had been a nice gesture, and had made up for some of the snide remarks a few of them had made to her since finding out she had put herself on the *"auction block"* as Hilda Sanders had put it. Charise hadn't felt the desire to share her main reason—that she couldn't stand to see that no good Ethan Breckinridge even one more time. No one understood that except Beth Ann.

Thinking of her best friend and roommate, Charise let out a small sigh. She would miss her terribly, and that thought almost made her want to back out of the deal all together. But, Charise knew she couldn't do that—Beth Ann had already secured another girl to share the apartment and help with expenses.

No, there would be no turning back now. Her course was set. Her bags and trunk were packed, and waiting. All that was needed was her groom.

At precisely 9:30, Charise and Beth Ann walked the four blocks from the apartment to Central Station, and it being a Friday, the depot was congested with people anxious to leave the city for the weekend. June had turned out to be unusually hot and humid, even by Ohio Valley standards. Most wealthy city dwellers kept summer homes outside of the sweltering crowded downtown with its tall brick or stone buildings and cobblestone streets making everything feel even hotter. Those who didn't have that luxury were trying to escape to cooler areas for a bit of reprieve.

Charise didn't blame them one bit; matter of fact, she was happy to be leaving the overcrowded city for a more rural way of life.

Right on time, the Baltimore & Ohio southbound train pulled in on track four, and within minutes, passengers were coming down the long, narrow platform between the trains. As they stood together, the girls scanned each man walking toward them, looking for Finn's blue neckerchief. Charise had placed a large, purple feather in her hat to help him spot her. Finally, Beth Ann pointed, "There he is, look."

Walking along, carrying a worn carpetbag and wearing a suit that had seen better days and seemed a size or two smaller than it ought to have been, was a burley, broad shouldered, muscular man. He wore a bowler hat over wavy, light brown hair and sported a bushy beard and full mustache. A bright blue neckerchief was tied around his rather large right bicep. Confused, Charise stared at the man, thinking he didn't resemble the young man in the photograph at all.

"Mmm, I don't know, Beth...Finn told me he is clean shaven..."

The two watched as the man, who seemed to be a bit unsure of where to go, stood looking around at the crush of people heading to and away from the trains in the large station. It truly was quite chaotic. A man with a clipboard walked by, calling out the trains, destinations, and departure times to the passengers, clearly wishing to hurry them along so that the trains could keep to their tight schedules.

As the man in the bowler looked their way, Charise saw his brown eyes focus on the feather in her hat. Then, his gaze lowered to hers and he tentatively approached.

"Ma'am...you wouldn't be Miss Charise Willoughby by any chance...would you?"

Charise's heart somersaulted. *Finn lied to me! Or...at least he misrepresented himself. Oh Lord, this isn't good. What else did he tell me that wasn't true?*

Swallowing her disenchantment, she took a step toward him and put out one hand. "Yes, I'm Charise Willoughby—and this is my friend, Beth Ann Gilmore. I...I take it then, that...you are Phineas Maynard?"

The man set his case down, snatched off his hat with one hand, and reached to give her hand a cursory shake as he shook his head. "No, I'm not Finn—I'm his brother, Samuel."

The girls looked at one another, wide-eyed, and then back at the man.

Frowning, Charise blinked. "His *brother*? I'm afraid I don't underst—"

He smiled and gave a nod of complete understanding just

as someone bumped into him from behind. The harried traveler mumbled an apology as he juggled several heavy valises and tried to get around the three standing in his way. The man, Sam, glanced around at the crowds of hurrying passengers and motioned them over out of the flow of traffic.

"Let me explain."

"What in Heaven's name is a *proxy* bride?" Charise exclaimed after the man—who she now realized was, indeed, Finn's brother, Sam—explained that Finn had been injured and Sam had volunteered to come in his place. But, what he said after that had been quite shocking. He quickly explained what a marriage by proxy entailed.

"Is that even *legal*?" Beth Ann asked. The girls exchanged glances, as both of them were beginning to have some serious reservations about Charise's long-distance fiancé.

Sam couldn't help but deliver the same understanding smile and nod as before. "Yes, it is. Quite legal, in fact." At their dubious expressions, he hastened, "Oh, believe me, I know what you're thinking. Why, I hadn't heard of it *myself* until five days ago. But, rest assured, I sent a telegram to the county clerk here and he assured me that proxy marriages are legal in Kentucky, as well as in several other states. Their only stipulation in this state is that the marriage take place at the courthouse, not in a church, as it must be performed by a judge."

"A proxy marriage...and not even by a minister in a church?" Charise repeated, becoming more uncertain about it by the minute. "I...I just don't know..." she lamented, her visions of wearing her wedding dress and getting married by Pastor Barkley disintegrating like a block of ice in the summer sun.

Sam pressed his lips together and replaced his hat. Glancing around, he asked, "Ladies, would there be somewhere more...quiet...that we could go to discuss this? Believe me, my brother is quite anxious for you to become his bride, Miss Charise. It took me *and* the doc to hold him down, as he was determined to come himself, but..."

Charise shook her head, snapping herself out of the fog his words had plunged her into and glanced at Beth as she answered, "Yes, Mr. Maynard—"

"*Sam*, please."

"Yes, um...Sam. I had planned that Finn and I would spend the afternoon in the restaurant of the Hotel Victoria, which is just two blocks away. They have wonderful food there and I had thought perhaps Finn and I could spend our wedding night—" she stopped, her face turning a bit pink as Sam grinned at her meaning.

"Hotel Victoria it is. Ladies," he leaned down to grasp

his valise, "Lead the way."

Charise turned to vacate the platform, leaning close to Beth and whispering, "Please say you'll come with us to the hotel!"

Beth's eyes rounded for a moment, but then she gave an answering nod.

Charise said over her shoulder to Sam as they negotiated through the doors to the large lobby of the depot, "We'll walk, if that's all right Mr...Sam. It's not far."

Sam chuckled. "Walkin' sounds fine, Miss Charise. I've been sittin' for five days. Was startin' to feel like I was becomin' part of the wooden seats on those trains."

"Is Finn truly going to be all right?" Charise asked his brother over their wonderful lunch of mutton chops, mashed potatoes and gravy, cabbage, and mince pie for dessert.

Once they had settled into their seats and ordered, Sam had begun to explain in detail how Finn's accident had happened—prompting gasps and expressions of sympathy from both girls—and that Sam felt terribly guilty that his brother had been injured in his mill. Then he went on to tell what the doctor had said, and how upset Finn had been that he wouldn't be able to make the trip himself—*and* his concern over the fact that he knew she had given up her job and her apartment in preparation for leaving town with him to start their marriage.

"Oh sure," he answered her question. "Doc Reeves says he'll be fine as long as he takes it easy and stays off that leg. The main worry was the concussion, but there was a telegram waiting for me at the last stop which said he was over that, thank the Lord."

As they finished up their lunch, Sam answered every question either of the girls had, and volunteered information as well—except for why Finn was insisting that the marriage take place immediately rather than waiting for her to travel to Nebraska. On that point he was a bit vague, merely hinting that Finn was afraid that Charise would either bow out of the deal or have second thoughts.

For a few moments, Charise found herself wondering if Finn actually existed, or if this could be a ploy to get her away and do her harm, although she felt no warning bells of threat or danger in Sam's presence. Sam seemed to read those very things in her expression and hastened to reassure her that his brother suspected she might feel uneasy about the change in plans and he merely wanted to help her feel secure.

Finally, pushing back his plate, Sam wiped his beard with a linen napkin and smiled at Charise across the table.

"Well, Miss Charise? Will you have my brother in holy

matrimony, by proxy?"

Charise and Beth Ann met one another's eyes for a silent discussion. Charise raised an eyebrow at her friend, hoping for some advice, but Beth Ann, eyes like saucers, could only shake her head and shrug. It was obvious that Beth didn't want to stand in her way, *nor* take responsibility in case things went south. Truly, something like this was a big decision, and Charise knew she needed to trust her instincts. It was a concern that she wouldn't even get to meet her groom before the marriage took place, but his brother had shared many stories about him to help ease her mind.

Shutting her eyes, Charise said a quick, silent prayer for guidance, waited for several breaths, and as a feeling of peace began to fill her heart, she opened her eyes and smiled at her intended's brother.

"Yes, Sam. I accept your terms. I will become your brother's proxy bride."

Sam let out a yelp and then clamped a hand over his mouth and hunched his shoulders as the girls laughed and diners nearby looked over and gave the trio odd looks.

"Speaking for my brother," Sam grinned, "I say thank you, ma'am. Now, what shall be our course of action?"

It was decided that Sam would take a room at the Hotel

Victoria to, in his words, scour the grime of six hundred miles of train travel off his person, and would meet the girls on the steps of the courthouse at two o'clock. As they would need another witness, Beth Ann had persuaded her long-time beau, Stanley Clabor, to act as Sam, or rather Finn's, best man.

Charise had to fight off the disappointment that her romantic plans for her wedding day had flown out the window faster than a bullet shot from a Kentucky long rifle. Her beautiful wedding dress that she'd spent dozens of hours making...her mother's cameo...all of the customary traditions like something old, new, borrowed and blue...a bouquet...being married by the minister she had known all her life...a lovely cake and reception... All of that seemed kind of silly in the face of her saying vows with a stand-in for her actual groom—a groom she hasn't even met face to face. It placated her a bit that Sam confessed to Finn's fear that, if he'd asked her to wait, another man might come along and sweep her off her feet. So, though it may seem petulant, she chose to chuck all of it and just get married in the blue silk day dress.

*Perhaps Finn and I can have a **real** wedding, in church, in Nebraska...* Well, she wouldn't worry about that now, and would cross that bridge when she came to it. For now, she had to get on with the business of legally becoming Mrs. Phineas Maynard.

Promptly at two o'clock, Sam stepped out of a two-wheeled hansom cab pulled by an old brown and gray nag, and started up the steps toward them as they waited on the landing at the top. Charise's heart warmed as she observed he was wearing a nicer suit, and saw what he was clutching in one hand—a bouquet of flowers.

When he reached them, a bit out of breath, Sam noticed the direction of her eyes and he handed the flowers to her with a small bow. "Finn made me promise to get you a bouquet from somewhere for you to carry for the ceremony—even if I had to pluck flowers out of somebody's yard," he laughed. "But luckily, I found a flower vendor on the sidewalk outside the hotel."

Pausing, he looked at the other couple, and inclined his head in greeting, then gently grasped Charise's elbow as he guided her over several feet for a private talk.

"Miss Charise, a couple of things...I'm gonna put a ring on your finger today, but it won't be your real one. Finn is gonna give you our mother's wedding ring, but he wants to be the one to put that on you hisself, so...don't be disappointed in the ring. All right? And..." he hesitated for a few seconds before adding, "He wanted you to know that once I get you to Brownville, our friends are gonna throw a shindig for you both. In case I didn't say it, he wanted you to know how sorry he is that he got hurt and messed up the plans. He said to tell you he promises to make it up to you if it takes the rest of your lives together."

Again, Charise warmed at the thoughtfulness of these brothers from Nebraska. If this was an example of their care and concern for her, she knew she was doing the right thing and putting herself into good hands. With an appreciative smile and nod, she said, "Thank you, Sam." She slid her hand into the crook of his arm and added, "Shall we proceed, Mr. Maynard?"

Sam gave her a smile that stretched from his twinkling blue eyes to his bushy brown beard as he said, "At your service, ma'am."

The next two hours went by quickly.

They carried on a quiet conversation as they stood in line to apply for the marriage license, and had to tell the clerk twice that they needed a proxy marriage. The hapless young man had never done that before and wasn't sure what was needed. Then, they waited until Judge Noah Perry, the official that would solemnize the marriage, finished with prior business.

Finally, the four of them were standing in front of the judge's tall, elaborately carved oak bench and looking up at him expectantly. He had taken out a white handkerchief and had set to cleaning his wire-rimmed glasses. His hair, the four noticed as they silently waited, had receded so far, he now only had curly, salt and pepper hair at the very back of his head, a full six-inch beard and a gray mustache, and his dark blue suit was covered by a black judge's robe.

He fitted his glasses around his ears and looked down at them as he ran his hand over his whiskers. "I'm Judge Noah Perry, and since this is only the second proxy marriage I have solemnized, I need to get the particulars straight. Now, Mister..." he paused as he picked up a file and read the paperwork Sam had provided, "Samuel Maynard. You are the groom's brother, is that correct?"

"Yes, your honor. My brother, Phineas, was injured back home in Nebraska. He got a bad concussion and broke his leg, and he asked me to stand in for him. It's all there in the papers, signed by our town doctor and by Finn," he added as he stepped forward. The judge spent a brief time reading and then speared Sam with a look over top of his glasses. "May I ask why Miss Willoughby didn't just go to your brother and get married in Nebraska? Isn't that what most mail-order-brides do?"

Sam cleared his throat and sent an apologetic glance toward Charise that made her heart hitch nervously. *What in the world is he going to say?* Taking a step closer toward Judge Perry, he murmured, "Well, Judge...your honor, sir...it's like this..." he paused and gave a small, uncomfortable shrug, reaching up to unconsciously tug at his collar. "My brother, well...he had sent for a mail-order-bride once before and...she took his money for the tickets, but went to another man, so...this time around, he wasn't takin' no chances," he raised his eyebrows and met the judge's eyes full on, man to man. Judge Perry gave a nod of understanding.

"I see." He finished looking over the paperwork and satisfied that all was in order, he turned his attention to Charise, offering her a kind smile.

"Young lady, this situation—your groom's brother standing in for him in a proxy marriage—is all right with you? As they say—speak now or forever hold your piece."

Charise fought back a feeling of uneasiness, but managed to answer, "Yes, your honor."

Having dreaded the idea of traveling to a far away state as a mail-order-bride, it had relieved her mind considerably when Finn had written her that he would travel to Louisville and they would be married before she had to leave her home and everything familiar. As Finn had neglected to tell her about his previous mail-order-bride and what she had done, Charise now felt several emotions sweep over her simultaneously—sympathy for him, but offense that he would harbor any thoughts that she, herself, might do such a thing. The deciding factor for her decision to go through with a proxy marriage had been that with a legal marriage license in her possession, she wouldn't be traveling to a strange place with a man she didn't really know and taking a chance that all was not as had been declared. Like any normal woman, her greatest fear was being stranded in a far away place as a single girl with no recourse or provision.

"And these two are your witnesses?" the judge continued.

"Yes, sir," Beth Ann and Stanley replied in unison and then stated their full names.

With a satisfied nod, he began the proceedings.

"All right then. You two stand there facing one another," he pointed to the space immediately in front of his bench, "and Mr. Maynard, take Miss Willoughby's hands." Sam did so. The judge cleared his throat and Charise felt herself start to tremble. Sam squeezed her hands and she met his eyes, his wink helping to alleviate a bit of the stress.

"We are gathered here today in the presence of these witnesses to join in holy matrimony Miss Charise Willoughby and Mr. Phineas Maynard by proxy," he began. Addressing Charise, he said, "Charise Olivia Willoughby, do you take the man, Phineas Oliver Maynard, to be your lawfully wedded husband, and with him to live together in holy matrimony pursuant to the laws of God and this state?"

Charise gripped her bouquet and moistened suddenly dry lips when the judge mentioned that the marriage would be legal in God's eyes. *Lord, am I doing the right thing? If not...stop me! Make the ceiling fall in or something...*

Allowing several seconds for Divine intervention, she vowed silently, *Well all right then, Lord. Here goes...*

She took a deep breath. "I do."

"Do you promise to love Phineas, comfort him, honor and obey him and keep him both in sickness and in health, and forsaking all others, keep yourself only unto him, so long as you both shall live?"

"I do."

The judge nodded and addressed Sam. "Mr. Samuel Maynard. Acting on behalf of, and in full consent and understanding and duly signed permission from your brother, Phineas Maynard, do you take this woman to be his lawfully wedded wife, to have and to hold from this day forward, for better or for worse, for richer for poorer, in sickness and in health, to love and to cherish till death do you—or rather *he*—do part?"

Without a second of hesitation, Sam answered with a strong, "I do."

"Is there a ring?"

"Yes, your honor," Sam said, quickly producing a plain gold band from his pocket and slipping it onto Charise's outstretched, trembling finger as the judge led Sam in the vow of the ring.

"Then by virtue of the authority vested in me by the state

of Kentucky, I hereby pronounce you husband and wife. Mr. Maynard, you may, uh...kiss your brother's bride," he said with a chuckle.

Charise's eyes widened and her heart leaped into racing speed as Sam smiled kindly and leaned forward, only to veer off at the very last second to place a sweet, soft, warm, lips-surrounded-by-whiskers kiss to her cheek, just to the left of her lips. He whispered in her ear, "Finny told me he'd skin me alive if I kissed you before he got to," he chuckled. She felt herself blush.

At that instant, she had an inkling that she was going to have her hands full with the Maynard brothers...her *two* husbands.

Chapter 4

Brooding, Finn stood propped against the wall next to one of the second floor windows above his barbershop, steadied by a pair of rough-hewn crutches.

Today was the day. *Finally.* It had been eleven long days since Finn had sent his brother to fetch...and *marry*...his fiancée.

Ignoring the throbbing in his leg, caused by standing far too long and making the blasted thing swell, he stared anxiously down the wide expanse of hard-packed dirt known as Main Street toward the far edge of town where the railroad tracks crossed.

"Eleven days?" he let out a snort of disgust. *Seems like eleven years.* Idly, he watched as people went about their business on the street below and thought back over what had, at times, felt like a prison sentence.

At first, the doctor had made him stay in bed and rest until all evidence of his concussion had disappeared. Although he had griped and groused like an old bear, he had complied.

The dizziness and headaches, especially those that came each time he needed to sit up and awkwardly make use of the chamber pot, blessedly stopped assailing him after several days.

He'd always hated those things—chamber pots—preferring to make the trek outside to the outhouse even in inclement weather. But making use of it with one of his legs encased in a heavy, awkward cast just barely qualified as being within the realm of possibility. That indignity, combined with the humiliation of Elvira Davis volunteering to come by each day to empty the vile receptacle, see to his needs and bring him food, just about made him want to jump out a window. Then there was the inescapable torture of Elvira's penchant to fill the air with mind-numbing small talk. She had managed to transform his normally peaceful home into a house of mental purgatory. Truly, he feared that if his enforced confinement lasted one more day, it would push him over the edge of his endurance.

He shook his head and determinedly set his mind on something else.

There had been daily visits from Toby, the young man who had caused the accident, begging Finn to forgive him. It seemed no matter what Finn said to him, the youngster was determined to beat himself over the head. Each day, he tried to a near harmfully persistent degree to assist Finn, either by helping him to stand, or carry things around, but it was as if the poor lad had two left feet and two left hands, as he was forever dropping or tripping about the room. Finn silently wondered why his brother had *ever* thought the mill a good choice in which young Toby could apprentice for a future profession.

And if that wasn't enough, he'd kept imagining all sorts of scenarios that could and might happen once Sam reached Louisville. Charise could tell him that she had changed her mind. She could be adamantly opposed to the idea of a proxy marriage, so much so that she washed her hands of the Maynard brothers completely. Matter of fact, Charise balking at the proxy idea was the very reason he hadn't sent her a telegram broaching that subject ahead of time. He figured Sam would have more success asking her in person—his brother could be most persuasive when he chose.

Alas, if he were honest, another recurring fear was that Charise, in reality, wasn't anything like her picture, but more resembled a screeching fishwife. His thoughts then bounced to the inevitable worry that she was planning on using his money for some other reason.

Once the days had gone by and Sam replied to the telegram Doc Reeves had sent to the Clarksville, Indiana station, things had smoothed out into just the frustration of waiting.

Somehow, he had survived the delay. Sam and Charise were due in on the three o'clock train. Now, with the anticipation of it all, Finn felt as if he were on the brink of jumping out of his skin.

From his vantage point in the upper window he couldn't see the depot itself, but he would be able to see when they were coming, as they would have to walk down the street to get to his shop.

It galled him that he couldn't go to the depot to meet her. She was his *wife* doggone it! His *wife*! The telegram announcing that welcome news was stashed protectively in the pocket of his trousers. He had taken it out and read it countless times since Charlie Cooper, the telegraph operator, had hoofed it over. Oh, how Finn wished he was healed and whole, able to stand on the depot platform with flowers in hand, waiting to sweep Charise into his arms with an amorous Nebraska *hello!*

But he was practically a prisoner in his rooms because of the inane design of the interior stairs to the second floor—which were circular. Built thusly to save space in the narrow building, the treads turned in such a tight circle inside a four by four box that there was *no way* he would be able to navigate them in the despised cast. Funny how the design of the steps had never bothered him before—it had never occurred to him that they would ever be a problem. How quickly things can change!

Sam sure had been right, he fumed, *I should have taken the bull by the horns and rebuilt one of the outside staircases, at least the one up to the back porch. Ah well, as they say, hindsight is 2020. But that will sure be the first project I take on once I get this stupid cast off...*

Just then on the street below, Kenny and Johanna Bruner, friends he had known since their school days, rolled slowly by in their wagon.

From his bird's-eye view, Finn watched as Kenny leaned over to gently bump shoulders with his wife and murmur something while motioning with his head toward Finn's shop. Johanna chuckled and turned her head toward him, raising one hand to lovingly caress his scruffy cheek. She murmured something and Kenny tipped his head back and laughed. Finn wondered if they were talking about the barbershop being closed, thereby rendering Kenny unable to receive his weekly shave. But, the *look* the couple shared, as if they were communicating without words, made Finn long for that same thing with his new bride. Would Charise look at him like that one day? A look filled with love and that private knowledge of one another that only comes as husband and wife?

Finn ground his teeth together and fumed. *What a way to*

start a marriage! Me trapped up here like a rat in a cage and my bride having to step and fetch for me. That thought vexed him to no end. He'd had so many plans for their first weeks and months as a married couple, once they had returned from Louisville and she had settled in as his wife. He had so looked forward to proudly escorting her around town to meet everyone, with her hand securely tucked into the crook of his arm as they strolled along. He'd pictured taking her down to the Blue Bird Café to eat dinner...having dinner alone in their rooms by candlelight...walking her to church the first Sunday after her arrival...squiring her on picnics out in the open land past the edge of town, or maybe to his favorite little stretch of beach at the river's edge...

But noooo, I had to go and break my fool leg, forcing her to marry what amounts to an invalid—a temporary invalid, true, but an invalid nonetheless. How would she be able to think of him as her protector and man of the house if he couldn't even transport himself? *Aggghh!*

And then, there was the thought that his brother—strong, good looking, muscular, lumberjack Sam, had spoken *vows* with her and had been traveling with her alone for five days! The still sane part of his brain once again mentioned that Charise and Sam were traveling with thirty or so other people in the various passenger cars on the journey. *Still*, his fuming mind argued, *at this point, my **brother** knows my bride better than I do!* He just hoped Sam had taken him seriously when he'd ordered him not to kiss Charise on the lips during the wedding ceremony. *If I find out he did, so help me, I'll skin...*

The unmistakable sound of a train whistle broke into his self-imposed torture and he nearly lost his balance as he leaned into the window to catch a glimpse of the cars as they passed by the end of the street.

Unable to stop himself, he quickly laid his crutches aside and fumbled with the large, double-hung window, managing to push it up and thereby allowing enough room to park himself safely on the sill. *Ok, now...it's only a matter of minutes and she'll be coming down the street to me. And it's about time!*

"End of the line, Brownville!" the conductor announced as the engine chugged toward a small but neat, red brick depot.

Charise had been on pins and needles since they had boarded in Nebraska City for the last thirty miles of their five day journey.

"You ready to meet your husband, Mrs. Maynard?"

Hearing her new name spoken aloud gave Charise a delicious little tingle all over.

Turning her head to flash a smile at her ever-solicitous

traveling companion, she watched as he placed his bowler firmly on his head and turned warm, brown eyes twinkling with mirth her way. A shiver of anticipation and a bit of anxious fear of the unknown shimmered down her spine, but she took in a deep breath and nodded.

Over the last five days, Sam had become like the brother she always wished to have had as they shared their life stories, meals, and comfortable silences while the miles rolled along outside of the dusty train car windows.

The first thing he'd done, in big brother fashion, had happened right outside the courthouse after the wedding.

Descending the steps, wouldn't you know, they had come face to face with none other than her ex-fiancé, Ethan Breckinridge, and his high-society wife. True to form, Ethan looked the group over and sneered sarcastically.

"Well, well, Miss Willoughby, what do we have here? Is this the mail-order *beau* I heard you'd responded to?" He gave Sam the once over. "He's rather a burley character. Really, Char, I knew you were lamenting our breakup, but aren't you scraping the bottom of the barrel with this one?" Charise had opened her mouth to snap a retort, but in the blink of an eye, Ethan found himself on the ground, looking up wide-eyed at a boiling mad Sam and rubbing a sore jaw while his wife squealed and bent to his aid.

Words unnecessary, as his fist had spoken for him, Sam

had taken Charise by the elbow and glared down at the prostrate man while steering her around and on down the street, mumbling, "Talk to my sister-in-law like that, will he?" Beth Ann and Stanley had laughed and enjoyed themselves, while Charise reveled in the warmth of being defended. She hadn't even looked back, but continued on down the street with her head held high. It had been a great feeling.

There were times on the trip when Sam had put himself between Charise and others who may or may not have had nefarious intentions, but he was taking no chances. By the second day, Charise knew she couldn't have had a better escort unless it had been her husband, himself.

Now, mistaking her expression as concern over his comment, Sam reached to pat one of her hands as it clutched the back of the seat directly in front of theirs and gave her one of his customary winks. "Trust me, sister-in-law—something tells me this match was arranged in heaven. And...if I thought that brother of mine would do anything to hurt you, I'd have never agreed to go halfway across the country and fetch you for him. However..." he paused with a snicker. "Finn can be a bear sometimes when he's feeling under the weather. Ma always said he made a lousy patient, so...be prepared. If I was a bettin' man, I'd say about now he's chompin' at the bit to get that cast off his leg."

The train wheels screeched to a stop then and the

passengers heard the familiar hiss of releasing steam before they each stood to their feet and began gathering their belongings.

Stepping down the metal treads and onto the rough wooden landing, Charise looked to her left and saw where the tracks really did end about twenty feet past the edge of the platform. Sam had explained how the Midland Pacific Railroad had only extended the Nebraska City leg to Brownville a mere three months prior. She had literally gone to the end of the line! That thought gave her another small shiver of anticipation.

Once Sam had directed the offloading of her trunk and bags, he commenced with escorting her to her new home. On the journey, he had regaled her with stories of the town and its people, therefore Charise had been prepared for a tiny hamlet, having grown up accustomed to living in a city the size and scope of Louisville, but she was pleasantly surprised at Brownville's size. It had a main street with four cross streets dissecting it, and then Sam pointed north and explained that as Brownville was a port city on the Missouri River, it had a good sized docking area for its brisk steamboat trade and a sizable hill on which the wealthier businessmen had built homes above the flood plain. At the top of the hill, Main Street spread out with one and two story brick or timber buildings positioned side-by-side, with overhangs and wooden boardwalks running the length.

As they turned onto the street, Charise saw quite a few people going about their day strolling along the boardwalks, rolling along in wagons, or riding horseback. She could see storefront signs for Hodges Mercantile, a newspaper office—The Nebraska Advertiser, the Brownville Bank, Bortner Drug Store, a blacksmith, a gunsmith, several churches, and just as many saloons—and this was just on Main Street. Sam indicated the direction of the brickyard, the school, his sawmill and lumberyard, and many other businesses. Her mind spun trying to remember it all.

"Up ahead is Finn's barbershop," Sam murmured as they walked along.

Training her eyes in the direction Sam was now pointing, Charise suddenly gasped, "Sam! Is...is that Finn up in the window?"

Sam looked again and chuckled, shaking his head. "Yep. The darn fool, hanging out the window like that. He's liable to fall out and break the other leg."

Charise shot a look at her companion. "Oh, don't say that!" she gasped as she quickened her pace.

The moment had arrived—she was about to meet the man she had wed.

Finn hung onto the window frame as he leaned out the

aperture to watch his bride and his brother walk down the street toward him. She had caught his eye the moment the two of them had turned the corner onto Main Street and he'd lost his breath at her loveliness. Wearing a maroon colored outfit that looked to be in fashion, at least more so than most of the ladies in town wore on a weekday, she carried a matching parasol trimmed with chainette fringe over one shoulder and was nodding as Sam pointed out things of interest during their stroll up the street.

Although he couldn't see her features yet, her trim figure and tiny, corseted waist gave him a good first impression. Even from that distance, he could tell she was no fishwife. Corroboration of this came by way of several men along the route aiming grins and tipping their hats to her in greeting.

Then he saw Sam aim his finger in his direction and she turned her head, hesitating when she saw him perched in the window. The next thing Finn knew, his bride was hurrying—*running*—up the street toward him with her skirts swishing and her parasol bobbing. He nearly let go of his handhold in exhilaration.

Seconds later, she was standing on the wooden sidewalk below him, gazing up with blatant concern while his winded brother merely chuckled by her side.

"Phineas?" she asked as she directed her vivacious stare his way, and he was immediately pleased with the cadence of her voice—soft, not too high or nasally, and most of all, full of care and concern.

He couldn't look away from her lovely face, nor those deep brown eyes, sparkling up at him. Heck, the word lovely didn't do her justice—she was gorgeous! *How did the fellas in Louisville manage to pass up this gem?* He cleared his throat and tried to rein in his galloping pulse.

"Um, yeah, I'm Finn," he managed to answer, after which both of them merely continued to stare at one another. Dare he hope that she was as pleased with his appearance as he was with hers? *Ahh, but how can she be, with me leaning here with this ridiculous cast on, and one leg of my trousers rolled up...*

Finally, after a small crowd of onlookers began to gather, Sam laughed and "*Ehemmm'd*", suggesting to Charise that they go on inside so that she could give her groom a proper greeting.

She seemed to blush as she glanced around at their impromptu audience and allowed Sam to escort her inside. Much to Finn's chagrin, that meant she was out of his sight.

He sat perfectly still for a few heartbeats as he contemplated the fact that she was finally here until a voice from down below hollered, "Don't fall out the window, there, Finny boy! You might break both your arms, and then you won't be able to give your new bride a hug and kiss!"

The voice belonged to Cyrus Ames, of course, who else.

The group that had gathered had a good laugh at Finn's expense before he managed to gather his crutches and push himself into a standing position. For good measure, he slammed the window shut against the cackles and catcalls.

Charise felt her face heat with embarrassment over the ribbing Finn was taking as Sam ushered her inside through a matching pair of tall, narrow center doors, and only managed to grab a quick look at the exterior of her new home.

The brick building sported a shallow front alcove with three half-circle arches supported in the middle by two brick pillars, all painted a nice, clean white. Immediately above the arches were three corresponding domed windows overlooking the street below, one of which Finn had been sitting in. A large red, white and blue striped barber's pole was attached to the outer wall next to the entrance, its fading colors indicating its age.

She found herself intrigued by her husband's shop and living quarters. Although she knew many people back home who had lived above their businesses, she had never imagined herself as a shopkeeper's wife and she found she liked the idea. Her husband would never be far from her—out on the range, or out in the fields—if she needed him for something. The building was much bigger than she had imagined—and at first glance it seemed to be well maintained.

Stepping inside, she paused to allow her eyes to adjust to the dim light and the first thing she noticed was that the hardwood floor was scuffed and scarred, and seemed dusty, as if it hadn't been swept in a good while. The cream colored walls needed a fresh coat of paint and the scratched and marred wood grain wainscoting along the bottom third of the walls could have done with an application of fresh varnish.

Along the left wall stood an expansive, waist high counter area, that resembled a...bar? Its surface was stacked with crates and indefinable items. Charise turned her head to meet Sam's eyes in silent question and he smiled indulgently. "This building used to be a tavern called the Lone Tree Saloon, and yep, that was the bar. Finn'll tell you all about it," was all he would say.

Looking around, Charise saw that adjacent to the bar was the area where Finn did his barbering, consisting of various pieces of mismatched furniture, including a dry sink and a marble topped chest with drawers and a mirror. A small sign on the chest informed customers of the prices—haircuts twenty-five cents, bald heads fifteen cents, and shaves ten cents. A large potbelly stove sat unused on the hot June day. There were shelves on one wall filled with jars and tins containing various concoctions, the likes of which Charise had no clue.

In the center sat the barber chair itself, slightly resembling a throne, sporting burgundy velvet cushions, armrests carved with the likeness of a growling cougar, and a razor strop hanging by a string. A well-worn footrest was attached to the front. Her eyes took in what was obviously a waiting area with a bench and several wooden, straight-back chairs that divided the shop area from the rest of the extensive space.

Beyond this, about halfway down the lengthy wall, was what looked like a medium sized closet. The door to that was open and upon glancing inside, Charise saw a compact, winding stairway leading up to the second floor.

"That's the steps you told me about...and why Finn is a prisoner in his own home right now," she spoke quietly to her companion.

"Yep," he snickered. "This building used to have a big staircase running up the outside wall on the left, but it was rotted and unsafe, so he tore it down. Besides that, there was also a set of steps going up to the back porch, but those were bad, too. I told him he needed to go ahead and rebuild one of those right away, but he kept putting it off, saying he could get by with the steps in here for a while. I bet now he wishes he'd listened to me."

She sent him a smile and glancing around, she couldn't help but get a few ideas on how to tidy up the area, and use the long, narrow space to better advantage.

"Come on, I want to show you something," he encouraged as he rested one hand at the small of her back to guide her toward a door in the back wall. Charise gave a sidelong look at a mysterious, cumbersome mound of what, she couldn't tell, as it was covered up with a dusty tarp.

They reached the door, above which was a sign that read *Bath*. Another sign on the wall adjacent to it proclaimed that hot baths were twenty-five cents—soap and towel extra.

Sam opened the door leading into a vestibule, which contained an outer egress, and to the right, yet another door that stood open. Peeking inside, Charise discovered a good-sized bathing room containing a cast iron and porcelain claw foot tub along the back wall, next to which stood a small sink—with a hand pump for water! Delighted to find her new home contained such a luxury, Charise let out a pleased gasp.

"Oh Sam! A private bathing room! With a water pump!" she was enthused as she turned her head to grin at her brother-in-law. He had left that detail as a surprise and now chuckled at her reaction.

"Yep. The story of that tub's journey all the way from Chicago will have to wait for another time, though."

There was another wood stove in the corner, and a shelf on one wall that held towels, soap, and other bathing paraphernalia.

Sam gave her a few moments to look around, but when they both heard a thump from somewhere above, Sam cleared his throat. "C'mon, Finn's quarters are upstairs...and I think he's getting anxious to meet you," he snickered as he guided her back to the main room and toward the steps.

He started up and she unconsciously smoothed her hair and her skirts for her first face-to-face meeting with the man waiting at the top. Her groom. Her long-awaited husband...

Goodness! She didn't think she would be so nervous! In spite of everything Sam had told her, and all that Finn had written in his letters—her husband was still a virtual stranger to her. Once again, she hoped she had made the right decision sitting there in the restaurant of the Hotel Victoria. Too late now, she had the duly signed, legal marriage license residing safely inside her reticule.

Then as she came around the last few curving treads, holding the handrail with one hand and her skirts with the other, an upper hallway came into view. It was pleasant, with matching settees and small round tables on either side. Straight ahead was a door that led outside, presumably to what had been the outer staircase.

She reached the landing just as her new husband maneuvered around the corner of the hall on his crutches, an anxious gleam in his eyes.

Having seen him perched in the window and been unable to take her eyes from his, she now felt the exact same way. *Heavens to Betsy, he's handsome.* Truly, she was quite pleased with his looks and found herself feeling an instant attraction. She moved forward, and as she neared him, the first thing she realized was the truth of what Sam had said—the brothers looked nothing alike.

Finn was a little shorter and slighter in stature than his brother—but was by no means a small man. On the contrary, he had a nice, fit physique, wide in the shoulders and narrower at the hip. His hair was dark brown and wavy, almost curly, and nearly reached down to his collar. He had a fine masculine nose, a strong brow and chin, straight, white teeth, and midnight blue eyes, which were twinkling just then with a look that probably mirrored her own expression—pleased. Delicious tingles seemed to be racing up and down her spine as she allowed her eyes to drink their fill of Mr. Phineas Maynard.

Sam shoved his hands in his trouser pockets and rocked back on his feet, watching the brand new couple assess one another.

"Charise...meet Finn...your husband...the one I stood in proxy for..." He prompted, but neither moved.

"Finn, this here's your new wife," he tried again, but Finn merely stared as if transfixed.

Finally, Sam nudged his brother playfully. "Well, brother of mine—she's come over six hundred miles for ya. Get your head out of the clouds and greet her proper-like!"

Finn gave his brother a glance and cleared his throat, seeming to realize he had been staring. His cheeks even seemed a bit pink. Charise watched as he let go of his crutches and reached out to take her hand.

She moved hers to accept and when their fingers touched...a tingle shimmered up her arm at the contact.

Then, just as she opened her mouth to say hello—with a yelp, he fell flat on the floor at her feet!

CHAPTER 5

"**F**inn!" Charise squealed. "Good heavens, are you all right? Did you hurt your leg? Oh Sam, help him up, oh my goodness," his wife fretted on and on as her hands fluttered around him in near panic, only making Finn feel like a clumsy idiot.

Son of a b—bacon bit! What a way to meet my bride, Finn fumed as his brother helped him up off the floor, amidst Sam's chuckles and Charise's continued fussing.

"I'm all right, *dag nabbit*," he grumbled, unconsciously batting his bride's hands away as Sam hauled him upright, holding on as he steadied himself on his good leg. "Just lost my balance, is all," he added, hating that he was so helpless. He felt downright unmanned! Blast this stupid cast! He chanced a look at her face from under his lashes, but all he saw in her expression was concern. Still...

Why, oh why, did her first encounter with me have to consist of me making a darn fool out of myself, while she looks like a gorgeous gem, travel dust and all? And what was that...that tingle I felt when her fingers touched mine? Like the air crackling just before a lightning strike. Huh, yeah, lightning struck all right—knocked my feet right out from under me.

"Here, Sam, help him over to the settee," Charise instructed, making sure the cushions were out of the way while watching anxiously as Sam lowered Finn to the soft surface and positioned his cast just so.

"Brother, you scared ten years off my life with that little stunt," Sam huffed as he stood back. "You sure you're all right?"

Finn silently cursed the embarrassed heat he could feel infusing his face.

"Yeah. Unfortunately, that ain't the first time I tried to move and fell flat on my face," he admitted as he scrubbed his hands over his cheeks. He chanced another look at his bride when he felt her warmth as she sat down beside him.

She smiled softly. "Hello Finn. It seems an age that we've been waiting to meet...and now..." she paused and he watched as she scanned his face, her eyes trailing down his body to the heavy encumbrance of cast—extending all the way from his ankle to mid thigh—and back to his face. Reaching out with a delicate hand, she touched his cheek. "Although Sam told me about the cast, somehow I hadn't imagined it to be quite so large. Are you sure you are fine?

You didn't do...more damage?"

He managed a small smile as he lifted a hand and gently grasped hers, cocooning it between his own. Was he imagining it, or did he feel sparks every time they touched?

"Yeah, I'm fine. Doc said he made the stupid thing extra big and heavy because he knew I'd try and get around too soon." Remembering his actions during bouts of frustration, such as starting down the stairs, only to become wedged in place, forcing himself to be in need of rescue, he emitted a self-deprecating snicker and shook his head. "I hate that he was right."

Sam sat down on the opposite settee and chuckled. "He knows how you are, all right. No doubt he remembers that time you broke your arm fallin' out of old man Varner's apple tree—and then climbed it again, *with a cast on your arm*, and fell out again."

Finn flung a glare at his brother. "Stuff a sock in it, Sam. You'll make Charise here think she's married a chowderhead or somethin'."

Sam's head fell back with a guffaw and he ran a hand over his mustache and beard as if he were trying to control his mirth. Giving Finn that familiar *older brother* look that was both affectionate and teasing, he quipped, "Well, ain't ya?"

"You forget *why* I climbed that tree?"

Sam had the grace to flush a bit and look down. "Naw, I didn't forget. Not that you'd ever *let* me forget."

Charise looked back and forth between the men, one eyebrow rising in question. The brothers glanced at her and both pressed their lips shut, neither one willing to be one to spill the beans and explain.

Finn watched as his new wife sat back and crossed her arms over her chest. *Dang, she's lovely. I can't believe she's actually my wife!* He allowed his eyes to roam over her, starting with her lustrous, walnut brown hair, a few strands of which were coming loose from its long braid, and peeking out from under a smart hat that matched the color of her outfit. She had dark, defined eyebrows that framed chocolate brown eyes, which were fringed with black lashes. A straight nose and soft pink lips, which were now pursed in thought, complimented her smooth peaches and cream cheeks.

Then, she gave them both the *eye*, just like Ma Maynard used to do. "One of you want to tell me what this big *reason* was?" she murmured. Then, when neither one was forthcoming with information, she turned her stare Sam's way. "Sam?"

Finn was surprised Sam broke so easily, as he watched his brother reach up to tug at his collar before clearing his throat. "Aw, Charise, it's like this..." he paused with a huff. "I'd kinda...*borrowed* a kite from another kid..."

"Yeah," Finn interrupted, "*Borrowed*, only he didn't know about it. Not only that, it was the kid's birthday present and he and Sam used to get in scraps all the time—"

"Shut up, I'm tellin' this," Sam grumbled. Finn just grinned at him. "Anyway, it flew up into the branches of the tree and stuck there. Finny here, well, he climbed up to get it for me, but he fell before he reached it. Then that evening after all the hullaballoo of fixin' Finn's arm and all...that kid's pa came to the house and told our pa that he knew I took his boy's new kite and he wanted it back." Sam paused and winced. "After he left, pa gave me the lickin' of my life and said I'd better get the kite back to the kid by the next mornin' or I'd be in even more hot water...so, Finn climbed up there again. He got it that time...but comin' back down, he fell from the last branch. That time he didn't break anything, though," he added with a glint in his eyes as he met Charise's gaze.

She gave a nod, one eyebrow scrunched as she scrutinized the brothers. "All right. But...why didn't you climb up there and get it yourself?"

Enjoying himself, Finn relaxed back against the cushions and watched his brother squirm. "Yeah, *Sam*. Tell Charise why you didn't climb up there yourself."

Sam mumbled an off color word and glared at Finn as he mumbled, "'Cause I'm afraid of heights."

Finn's new wife sent a smile Sam's way as her tension eased a bit. "I can understand that...I don't fancy high places much myself. But I have to admit, Sam..." she paused and met Finn's amused eyes before turning back to his brother. "I didn't think you were afraid of *anything*."

Sam sat up a little straighter, puffing his chest out and sticking his bewhiskered chin forward a bit. "I'm *not*. 'Cept being up high," he admitted with a sheepish snicker.

Charise laughed at that, and Finn found himself enjoying her merriment. It wasn't an obnoxious cackle nor a childish giggle...more like a honeyed, dulcet tone, almost music to his ears. Something in the back of his heart knew he would spend the rest of his life trying to make her laugh, just so he could enjoy the sound. *No. Not only for that reason, but because her being happy will make me happy, as well.* He felt it, deep down in his bones. She moved a bit to get comfortable and he felt a shimmer of awareness skitter across his skin. Whew!

She chuckled again at something Sam said, but ruminating as he'd been about her looks and her sweet laughter, he'd missed it. She and Sam...they seemed like close friends already. Like sister and brother. Like...

As Finn sat looking back and forth between the two, absently rubbing his good knee that had taken the brunt of his fall as he watched his brother and his wife interact, he had to bite back a rush of green-eyed jealousy as thoughts from the previous week came flooding back to him...*my brother already knows my wife far better than I do...*

They'd been talking for over an hour. The guys had been regaling her with stories of their boyhood in Brownville, when the town was a newly wrought hamlet of only a dozen cabins and a few small places of business, and she had enjoyed every minute.

But now, Charise discreetly covered a yawn as the events of the last five days—and most specifically the past hour—caught up with her. She desperately needed to find a bed and fall into it for a good night's sleep that consisted of stillness and quiet, rather than rolling and pitching, ceaseless movement, and relentless noise.

Finn glanced her way and noticed. "Aww honey, I'm sorry. We've been sitting here jawing and you're about dead on your feet," he lamented. She tried to wave away his concern, but another yawn chose that moment to take over. Sam laughed at her attempts to conceal it.

"I think our girl here has had enough. Finn, want me to give her a quick tour of your quarters—" he stopped as Finn seemed to bristle.

"*I* can do it," her husband stated baldly. At her and Sam's startled expressions, he offered a crooked smile. "I promise, no more falling flat on my face. I can get around up here if I'm careful."

The two brother's eyes locked and held and Sam seemed to get a silent message; after which he clapped his hands on his knees and announced, "Well, I'll leave you to it, then, and get on home and make sure my mill is still in one piece."

Getting to his feet, he reached out and took Charise's hand as she stood. "Welcome to your new home, sister-in-law. I enjoyed the trip—but I admit, it's nice to be home—and not inside a big, rolling, fire breathing, smoke belching monster anymore."

She laughed at his description. "I wholeheartedly agree." Then feeling a rush of affection for her affable brother-in-law, she rose up on tiptoe and pressed a soft kiss to his burly cheek. "Thank you, Sam, for being the best escort a bride could ask for—not to mention..." she paused and gave Finn a mischievous twinkle, "a wonderful proxy groom."

Sam seemed to turn a bit pink in the cheeks at that, cleared his throat, and mumbled something about coming by the next day to check on them before disappearing down the winding steps.

And with that—she was alone with her new husband.

Time passed slowly as they peered into one another's eyes, each extremely conscious of the fact that they were, for all intents and purposes, *married.* Charise wasn't exactly sure what Finn expected or what he had planned for this, their first night as a married couple. She studied his expression as he sat up on the settee, carefully resting his casted leg against the floor.

Finn seemed to be able to read her unspoken question, as he smiled softly and reached over to grasp one of her hands.

"Um..." he began, moistening his lips as if he were trying to choose the right words. "I want to thank you, for agreeing to the proxy marriage and for becoming my wife—without even meeting me first. I want you to know that, once I'm on my feet again, I'd like to have a ceremony and repeat our vows—to *one another*. I know you had a wedding dress all made and all, but didn't get to use it..." he paused, looking deeply into her eyes. "Would you like that?"

She relaxed a smidgen and smiled. "Yes, I'd like that very much, and I'd hoped you'd feel that way. I'm afraid the solemnizing wasn't much of a ceremony back home...just a judge having us repeat some words. I admit that I was so nervous, I hardly remember anything I said," she added with a soft chuckle.

They remained as they were for a few moments, each deep in thought. And then Finn said, "Well, would you like to see your new home, Mrs. Maynard?"

She answered with a nod and stepped back to give him room as he took hold of his crutches, set his good leg firmly under him, and hefted himself up. Once he was balanced, he inclined his head to indicate for her to precede him, instructing her to turn right at the end of the entry hall.

"I don't know how much Sam told you about this building..." he began, and she answered over one shoulder, "Only that it used to be a tavern."

She noted he kept careful attention to his movements as he followed her, conveying with another nod for her to walk to a door at the end of a hallway that ran from the front to the back of the building. "That's right. And this floor was the hotel for the town."

"The hotel?" she asked, and he laughed.

"Small, I know, but it's true. But then, Brownville was quite small at the time it was built...in '60. I acquired the building six months ago and I've been slowly converting it. This room at the end I turned into a kitchen," he explained as she stepped through the doorway. Straight ahead was a backdoor to the outside and what must be the back porch Sam had mentioned, to the right of that stood a round table with some sort of green felt cloth on it, surrounded by four chairs—which Finn explained with a snicker had been one of the saloon's poker tables—a cast iron cook stove, a cupboard for dishes, pans and other necessities, and a large shelf for foodstuffs.

She walked on in, examining everything and finding it

quite adequate, with plenty of light from good-sized windows on each end. With a contented sigh, she turned and saw him observing her, so she blessed him with a smile. "This is wonderful. You should have seen the tiny kitchenette in the apartment that Beth Ann and I shared back home—just a corner of the parlor, really, with a small cook stove and table with two chairs. I feel like I'm in a mansion here," she added with a grin. He grinned back, obviously pleased with her response. But then a bit of a shadow spread over his eyes and he glanced around.

"Well, you can decorate it, or rearrange things, however suits you. This is your home now, too. I want you to be happy here. Give it that...*woman's touch,*" he offered and she gave a nod, intuitively knowing that her still calling Louisville *home* had bothered him a bit and she made a mental note to try and curb that habit.

Carefully turning to the right, he gestured for her to come with him and to open the door to the room next to the kitchen. Inside she saw a large, comfortable looking Empire settee with butter yellow velvet upholstery, a rocking chair, small table, along with several other items, and a brick fireplace on the far end. "This is the parlor." At her nod, he ushered her toward the next room down the hall.

"The hotel had six rooms to rent. One large one at the front of the building and five smaller ones," he explained. "I don't much use the front three right now, just have stuff stored in them. This room here is my...*our* bedroom."

She felt a tingle shoot through her veins at that word and the imaginings it conjured up as she opened the door to a pleasant room, the setting sun shining through a set of plain blue curtains and casting a warm glow over the double bed in the center. Several pieces of furniture took up the adjacent walls, including a chest with drawers, a large armoire, and a rocking chair. A potbelly stove sat ready in the corner. Covering the bed was a handmade patchwork quilt in dark blues, browns, and greens.

"My ma made the quilt for me when I got my first place..." he stopped and cleared his throat.

"It's very nice," Charise complimented as he gave a nod and smiled. She sensed he was feeling as anxious as she was.

They stood staring into one another's eyes, hearts pounding, and then Finn cleared his throat again. "Um...about tonight..." he began, and she moistened suddenly dry lips as he continued, "I've thought a lot about it and I figured...we don't have to hurry things. I mean, we can wait...get to know one another better before we...well, you know," he mumbled and Charise felt herself blush. He went on, "Besides...I'd like to wait until I can sweep you off your feet—on my own two feet—before we..."

Feeling her face flame even hotter, she looked down and then met his eyes. "I'd like that, too, Finn."

He drew in a big breath and then gave a firm nod of agreement. "That's settled then. So—for right now, you can sleep in here, and I'll sleep in the parlor on the settee."

That seemed wrong to Charise, and she immediately made to argue, "Oh, but Finn, I feel bad putting you out of your own bed—and to sleep on a settee sounds uncom—" she paused as he interrupted, firmly shaking his head.

"No, it's not. Matter of fact, I can get up and down easier from the settee than I can from the bed. Truly."

Placated, she let out a stuttering breath. "Oh, well, all right then. If you're sure."

Just then, they both heard a knocking on the door to the shop downstairs.

"I wonder who..." Finn grumbled, glancing down at his casted leg.

Charise understood immediately, and sent him a reassuring smile. "Don't worry. As of now, I start my duties. I'll go down and see who it is."

She turned and left him balancing in the bedroom doorway.

Charise could see several people through the glass panes of the narrow front doors as she unlocked the right hand side and swung it open.

"Yes?"

Standing there smiling were two males and two females—one a handsome woman of about thirty, with blue eyes and wavy brown hair peeking out from under a bonnet, and the other a woman of similar age, with frazzled reddish blonde hair and wide hazel eyes. With them were a young man who looked to be about sixteen, with bright red hair and light brown freckles dotting his fair skin, and an older man who appeared rather short in stature, with salt and pepper hair and wearing a railroad uniform and cap. The latter was holding the handle of a two-wheeled conveyance that bore her trunk and valises.

"Hello!" "Um, hi." "Ma'am." "Hey there." They each spoke at once.

Charise didn't know who to address first. One of the women cackled, Charise thought rather like a hen, and stuck her hand out. Then, she opened her mouth and, much like a Gatling gun, began to spew forth words with nary a pause to take a breath.

"Hey there, I'm Elvira Davis. You must be Finny's new proxy bride, Charise, am I right? Oh I know you are; he showed me the photograph you sent him. Why, you're even prettier in person than you looked in your portrait! I've been taking care of him since he broke his leg, you know. Oh, the poor man," she shook her head, tsking. "He was in such pain when it first happened. I felt so sorry for him, the poor dear. Why, he couldn't even get out of bed by himself, and I've been coming in each morning and taking care of his needs—you know—emptying the night time necessity, bringing him his food, and—"

"Elvira, I need to finish my business so's I can get back to the depot," the uniformed man interrupted, causing the woman to clamp her mouth shut with a snap and give him a glare.

Blinking from the barrage of words that had spewed out of the Elvira woman's mouth, Charise turned her attention to the man as he greeted her and said, "I'm Charlie Cooper, ma'am. I'm the telegraph operator and railroad ticket agent. I've got your trunk and things here."

"Oh...oh yes, please, bring them on inside," she requested, moving back out of his way and holding the door for him. The man hefted her trunk off the cart and set it inside the door, followed by her valises.

"Where would you like these, Miz Maynard?" he asked politely as the two women and the young man crowded in the door behind him. Charise allowed herself a few seconds of pure joy at hearing her new name before she collected her thoughts and demurely directed with one hand back toward the tight staircase. "I'm afraid I'll need them taken upstairs...if that's possible."

The man grimaced, but set his lips and gave an answering nod. "No problem," he mumbled as he carried the trunk over to the staircase door and started up, dragging it behind him as he occasionally let out a labored grunt and grumble with each step.

Charise pivoted back to the others and the second woman held out a hand.

"Hello Mrs. Maynard. My name is Dorothea Plasters. My husband, Dave, is the sheriff and I wanted to come and welcome you to town. And, it being your first evening and all...I brought some stew for you and Finn," she added, indicating the pot she held with potholders over its handles. "It's such a shame that Finn got injured right before your wedding," she added kindly.

Charise hadn't even noticed the pot in the woman's hands, and hurried to take it from her, but Mrs. Plasters shook her head and held it just out of Charise's reach. "Oh no, hon, I'll take it up. I know the way," she added with a smile and a mischievous sparkle in her bright blue eyes as she moved to maneuver around Charise.

She paused, however, and asked over her shoulder, "If that's all right?" Charise nodded numbly and the woman marched over to the stairway door and started up. *Oh my, what in the world did she mean by she knows the way?* Several reasons for the sheriff's *wife* being familiar with

Finn's quarters above his shop went through her mind, and none of them were nice. But...surely not...

Turning back, Charise only just then realized that the woman named Elvira had once again taken up her monologue, although the topics seemed to be bouncing from one thing to another. *My goodness, she doesn't even finish one thought or sentence before zigzagging to another!* It was positively enough to make one's head spin! Charise tried to smile at the bubbling woman, but then encountered the eyes of the young man, who was standing there gazing at her with a hangdog expression, his hands shoved deep into the pockets of his trousers.

"I'm...I'm Toby Keller, Mrs. Maynard. I'm...I'm the reason your husband got hurt," he mumbled over the flow of verbiage, his freckled face flaming bright red.

"Oh, yes. Sam told me about you...*and* that the accident was just that, an *accident*," Charise answered, hoping to help put the boy at ease.

He gave her a small smile before immediately shifting his attention to his feet and adding, "I...I just wanted you to know that if you need anything—anything at all—you just send somebody for me, if I'm not here already, that is," he murmured so low that Charise had a hard time hearing him over the barrage of nonsensical words flowing out of Elvira Davis' mouth. The boy tipped his cap at Charise and turned, fleeing out the doorway, leaving Charise utterly alone with the unstoppable word shooter. *Good heavens...being subjected to Elvira Davis is like being near a pot of water boiling over onto everything around it...* Charise hazily mused.

Bending, Charise picked up one of her carpetbags and the woman grabbed the other, babbling on and on about how the citizens of Brownville had been so excited the day the train first came to town. Wide-eyed, Charise could only nod, as there was no way to get a word in edgewise without blatantly interrupting the effervescent woman. She made her way to the stairway to follow their first two visitors, with Elvira tagging along at her heels.

Reaching the second floor, Charise just caught a glimpse of the edge of her trunk disappearing around the corner as Finn once again seated himself on one of the settees in the entry hall. Mrs. Plasters had paused to let him peek inside the pot of stew.

Charise moved to take her place at his side just as Elvira pushed past and plopped herself down next to him on the settee!

"Finny, I'm so happy that your new bride is here. Now, maybe you won't be so grouchy all the time," she gushed, elbowing his arm playfully. Turning to Charise, she continued right on, "Oh he's been terrible grumpy, trying to pace the floor with those God awful crutches, wishing the days to pass so that you and Sam would arrive. Let me tell *you*, why he just about—"

"*Elvira*," Finn cut in, commanding her attention.

She turned her head and smiled at him, blinking her eyes, obviously clueless. "Yes, Finny dear?"

Charise felt her breath catch and watched her husband absolutely blanch at the endearment. He opened his mouth to say something else, but the woman turned back to Charise.

"Now, I'll be here bright and early in the morning, just like always, and I'll take care of everything he needs. You won't have to worry yourself about anything, dear. Why, you can sleep late if you want to. Don't make no nevermind to me. I've got a key and I—"

"Miss Davis," Charise interjected, fuming. *That's the last straw. I'm Finn's wife and I'm here now—and there is no way I am going to let another woman take care of my husbands...**needs**.*

She'd had enough. She was tired, covered in grimy travel dust, and all she wanted to do was relax in her new home with her new husband. Summoning every bit of tact she possessed, Charise forced herself to smile and address Elvira. "I do thank you, and I'm sure Finn is grateful for all you've done for him since his injury, but...I'm here now, and I think I can handle things from now on. Don't you, Finn?"

she asked her husband, meeting his eyes and noting his pleased expression.

He merely gave a nod, but she could see he was trying his best not to all out grin. She had the feeling he was proud of how she was handling the situation.

Mrs. Plasters came around the corner from depositing the stew in the kitchen. Obviously having heard the exchange, she sent a wink Charise's way, took a firm hold on Elvira's arm and propelled her along as she called back over her shoulder, "Welcome to Brownville, again, Mrs. Maynard. We'll be seeing you soon. Come along, Elvira."

Charlie Cooper followed close behind. Charise descended the steps to see the visitors out and thank them for their help, locking the door firmly before once again ascending the narrow, winding stairway.

Alone again, the house was quiet as the newlyweds sent shy looks at one another with matching smiles.

"Well, Mrs. Maynard...shall we sample the stew?"

She smiled happily. "I think that's a fine idea, Mr. Maynard."

And so they did, enjoying their first meal together as husband and wife.

CHAPTER 6

The following morning as Charise stood at the kitchen table whipping up a batch of scrambled eggs, she fought back a yawn.

She had managed to get some sleep, but awakened early, dressed quietly, and hovered out in the hall as she peeked in at a sleeping Finn. She admired his dark, wavy hair all disheveled from his sleep, and observed how one arm was thrown over his face while the other was flung outward, suspended in mid air. Her eyes greedily took in his form that was only half covered by an old quilt. He'd removed his shirt during the night, and Charise felt herself blush as she remembered him telling her he usually slept in the buff. His broken leg, in its nefarious cast, was propped securely on the armrest, while the other was hidden just beneath the cover. She forced herself not to go in and risk the chance of waking him, but instead she had made her way into the dark kitchen.

Now, she was quite proud of herself that she had been able to get the fire started in the large cook stove and glanced over at it with a smile that quickly turned to a worried frown as thoughts cycled through her mind.

I hope Finn likes scrambled eggs...I forgot to ask him what he usually eats for breakfast. I hope he eats breakfast...most men do...right? I need to find out what his favorite meals are. Who would know? Maybe Sam? No, what am I thinking, I'll just ask Finn...he's such a nice man...and so handsome—even with that awful cast on his leg. I'm so glad I answered his advertisement for a mail-order-bride...

With a soft smile as she remembered the spark of attraction and awareness she felt each time they touched, Charise paused in her breakfast preparations to stare out the window next to the stove and allowed her thoughts to drift over the events of the previous evening.

They had enjoyed one another's company as well as the delicious stew Dorothea had thoughtfully provided. *What a kind woman,* Charise mused, thinking it would be nice to have a friend in town. She missed Beth Ann terribly, and made a mental note to find the time to write her friend a letter. At that moment, she couldn't imagine feeling friendship toward Elvira, but stranger things have happened. Indeed, she'd need to pray about that and ask for help.

Thinking of Dorothea again, Charise relived her surprise when Finn had shared that Dorothea Plasters, the wife of the town's sheriff, was also a cousin of the infamous outlaw Jesse James! *Good heavens, I can't imagine being related to a man who robbed trains and banks for a living.* She knew that people had different opinions about the robber. Even back in Louisville, whenever current escapades of Wild West outlaws were reported in the *Courier-Journal*, everyone seemed to want to voice their opinion on the degrees of evil or good in each one. Some people poured over each account as if they were reading a dime novel. None of it had seemed real to Charise—but now, to actually be friends with a family member of a renowned outlaw made everything come into sharp focus.

Shaking her head to get her thoughts back onto the task at hand, she set the bowl of eggs aside, went to the potato keeper, took out several, and began peeling and chopping to make hash browns. However, more memories of last evening insisted on floating through like a full-color dream. After they had finished their supper and cleaned up the dishes, she had helped Finn take what her roommate used to call a *bucket bath*—and once he'd taken off his shirt, she had found herself having a hard time stopping her eyes from straying to his muscled chest and torso with its fine sprinkling of masculine hair. Finally, shyness had gotten the better of her and she had retreated to the bedroom, taking her time finding clean clothing for him to put on in order to give him a chance to wash his...unmentionables.

At that memory, she felt her face pinken and she snickered in a whisper as she shook her head. It surely hadn't been what either of them had imagined for their first night together as man and wife!

She had made certain he was as comfortable as could be in the parlor, and then, after kissing him sweetly on the cheek, she had finally retired to the bedroom. Once there, despite the fact that she was worn out from days of travel and very little sleep, she had suddenly rallied with a second wind and an abundant amount of energy. So, she spent some time emptying her two carpetbags, neatly placing her clothing into the areas in the dresser and armoire that Finn had indicated were hers to use.

After that, she had quietly made her way down the winding steps to the bathing room for the first bath she'd had in days—and *oh* it had felt heavenly!

As she had luxuriated in the deep, hot water, she had paused to thank the Lord for matching her up with Finn. His home...*their* home now...was quite comfortable and she was confident that once Finn got back on his feet again, they would be able to create a nice life together.

Relaxing back against the tall rounded end of the tub and staring at the peeling paint on the bead board ceiling of the bathing room, she had indulged in some daydreaming about how their day-to-day lives might be in a few months. Would she and Finn fall in love...or just ease into a mutual affection for one another? Would she get with child right away?

Would she be able to make friends and truly think of Brownville as *home*? Life here would surely be different than her life had been in Louisville—recently *as well as* her early years, before everything had changed and her world had turned upside down.

Feeling nostalgic, Charise had slid down and wet her hair for washing. When she sat up, she reached for the bar of Honey Landing Lavender soap, one of a supply of special items she had brought from home—*correction, from Louisville*—and paused to take a sniff of the lovely fragrance before commencing her wash.

As she began to rub the smooth concoction into her long, dark tresses, the action reminded her of how her mother used to wash her hair as a child. Idly, she began to think back to her childhood, when she had lived with her beautiful mother, her dashing father, and two older brothers in an elegant stone home on Chestnut Street. Running her hand through the warm water and over the smooth, rounded porcelain of the tub, she mused, *we had a custom-made porcelain tub in our house, but I certainly took it for granted...*until everything she knew and loved was gone...

Her handsome, debonair father, Lovell Willoughby, had owned Willoughby Packet Company, which had operated several steamboats and made a quite prosperous living transporting goods from the southern states up to ports in the northeast. He was more than able to maintain an elegant home in a nice neighborhood, keep his wife in the latest fashions, and pay for the best schooling for his children. Her parents had been quite popular at the time, attending parties and dances and socializing with their peers. Lovell had even entertained the thought of running for public office.

However, when the war started, her father, a staunch Confederate, had pledged his steamers to the South's cause and eventually lost his ships and ultimately his business.

Charise's mother had been heartbroken and embarrassed by her husband's political bent, as she had been from northern Ohio and a firm unionist. Politics had been a source of more than one argument between the fashionable couple.

Divided ideologies seemed to be the norm in Louisville at the time. Kentucky, situated between three slave states and three free, was considered a border state and had declared itself neutral after the first shot was fired at Fort Sumter. Very few families in Louisville kept slaves before the war—those who did were mostly the owners of large tobacco plantations on the outskirts of the city. Working class folks in town didn't know what it was to have slaves do their work for them. Indeed, Charise's family had employed white servants from the less fortunate areas. Nevertheless, many pledged allegiance to the South and the Confederacy.

Louisville, however, soon became a major stronghold of union forces, even while a large amount of the city's population quietly sided with the Confederates. They were what people referred to as *closet patriots*—or as the North considered it—*closet rebels*.

Many families, such as the Willoughbys, found themselves divided. Once the war was in full swing, the Willoughby boys, Lovell, Jr. and Lawrence joined rival armies to fight for their opposing convictions. Sadly, both had been killed in early battles.

Thus, Charise's childhood had not been the stuff of little girl dreams but, rather, one of loss, sadness and disillusionment.

Without funds after the war, his ships lost, her father had taken to drinking and gambling, ultimately perishing in a carriage accident near the wharf. Their large home, her mother's jewelry, furs, and the majority of her extensive wardrobe, had been sold to pay outstanding debts and Charise and her mother had moved in with an elderly, widowed aunt who had a small house close to the river.

Soon after, Charise, who had always been handy with a needle and although only sixteen years of age, found a job in the alterations department of Fessenden & Stewart, a four-stories tall department store at Fourth & Jefferson. Her mother tried working, but having never held a job before, found it difficult to cope, and later that winter had succumbed to pneumonia after Charise found her wandering outside in a snowstorm.

The loss of each one of her family members had been hard, but Charise found that she had suffered the most from her mother's death. Even after nine years, it still brought on tears if she dwelled on it long.

Eventually her bath water had cooled and wiping the moisture from her eyes, Charise had purposely turned her thoughts back to her new marriage, with hopes and dreams for the future.

Suddenly, the sound of a thump in the next room brought Charise back to the present.

She placed the bowl to the side and wiped her hands on her apron as she hurried to check on her husband.

The door was ajar, just as she had left it the previous night so that she could hear if Finn called for her, and she peeked inside as she had earlier. He was sitting up, apparently getting ready to make use of the necessary. Catching a glimpse of his bare chest and some private areas on her new husband's body, she felt her face flame.

Stepping back quickly, she called through the opening, "Good morning, Finn. How are you this morning?"

She heard a grunt and some other noises she couldn't identify, and then her husband's voice answered, "I'm fine. Give me a few minutes, alright?"

Charise swallowed self-consciously and nodded, even though he couldn't see her. "Yes, of course. Um, Finn...are scrambled eggs, bacon and hash browns all right for breakfast?"

He answered immediately, which eased her mind. "That sounds great, Charise."

"All right...well...call if you need me to help you with...anything."

He replied with another grunt, and she hurried back to the kitchen to finish preparing breakfast.

Ten minutes later, just as Charise was placing the food on the table, Finn managed to open the door to the hall and maneuver into the kitchen. Watching him and remembering his fall the evening before, Charise had to clench her hands to keep herself from rushing to his side. She held back because she had the distinct impression that he wouldn't welcome being babied.

Instead, she smiled and turned a chair so that he could lower himself into it easily, and went ahead and took her seat. He was careful and no incidents happened as he made himself comfortable at the table. Surveying the food, he smiled with pleasure and met her eyes.

"Everything looks and smells wonderful, honey. I can't wait to dig in." Then, he reached out and took hold of her hand, bowing his head to say grace over the meal.

It warmed Charise's heart that her husband was a God fearing man of faith. In his simple prayer, he thanked the Lord for his new wife as well as her and Sam's safe trip across all those miles. He blessed the food and ended the prayer by asking God to bless their marriage and give them many years of happiness—and children—together. At that last item, Charise couldn't help but smile.

"Amen," she said when he finished. He was still holding her hand as she looked up entranced with his unwavering stare. His eyes were sparkling with happiness as he drew her hand to his lips and gave it a gentle kiss.

"I'm so happy you're here, Charise. Thank you for saying *yes*."

She let out a soft giggle as he wiggled his eyebrows. "I'm glad I'm here, too, Finn. And...you're welcome."

He let go of her hand, picking up his fork to tuck into his food, as he placed a large bite of eggs and potatoes in his mouth, and with a relishing moan, quipped, "Mmm mm, this is sure good. Think I'll keep ya."

Her mouth dropped open at that and her eyes flew to his, but then she chuckled as he winked.

So, my new husband is the teasing type...hmm...my brothers used to tease me like that. All right, I know how to play that game. She feigned relief and wiped pretend perspiration off her forehead with the back of one hand.

"Whew, that's a relief. I was *worried.*"

He let out a guffaw at that and took a drink of coffee. "I bet." Then as they both forked up another bite, their eyes met and Finn smiled again, his eyes twinkling. "Yep. I think things are going to work out just fine, Mrs. Maynard. Just fine."

Charise agreed wholeheartedly.

"Thank you, Toby," Finn heard Charise say from directly below where he sat on the back porch, his casted leg propped on a second kitchen chair. The young man had offered to do chores for Charise, and Finn had insisted she have the boy carry the used chamber pot to the outhouse. She seemed pleased and downright relieved to have the help.

"You're welcome, Miz Maynard," he heard the boy say, and then just as the lad came into view through the porch rail, he looked back over his shoulder at Charise and nearly tripped.

"Oh, be careful! Don't drop it!" he heard her caution as she probably pictured what a mess it would make if the boy were to drop the wretched thing. Finn watched anxiously as the young man stumbled forward but mercifully righted himself and held onto the metal receptacle. Finn was thankful it wasn't the ceramic variety.

The young man's pale, freckled face flamed red and he mumbled, "Don't worry ma'am, I got it," before shuffling away to attend to the task.

From his perch, he heard Charise chuckle and the swish of her skirts as she turned to make her way back inside the building. He imagined her shaking her head at the clumsy youth's antics.

A sense of peace and contentment settled over him and he couldn't help but allow a fine smile to spread across his face as it registered deep in his soul how much better things already seemed with Charise installed as mistress of his home.

Ahhhh, he sighed as he laid his head back and closed his eyes, remembering the previous evening—their first evening together as husband and wife—and how they just seemed to mesh. Already. Who would have thought?

Once they had finished eating Dorothea's delicious stew and chatted as Charise had washed the dishes—with him drying them as he sat at the table—Charise had offered to help him take a sponge bath...*what had she called it? Oh yeah, a bucket bath.* Well, whatever it was called, it had been a much less embarrassing event with Charise helping rather than Elvira.

They had spent some time relaxing and conversing in the parlor, during which he marveled at how they seemed to compliment one another's personalities so well, until finally he had insisted that she go on to bed and try and get some rest. He smiled softly as he remembered her gentle kiss to his cheek, and the warmth of her hand in his as they had bid one another good night.

After she'd left him alone, he had heard her shuffling around in the bedroom, albeit quietly, and he figured she was putting away her clothes. He'd smiled and nodded, understanding immediately that the tension and excitement of finally meeting one another had chased her fatigue right out the door.

Then, he had heard her footsteps as she had made her way downstairs. Even before he discerned the sound of a fire being made in the stove and the water being pumped, he had suspected she'd given in to the temptation to take a bath in his big, claw foot tub. He surely understood that, as he couldn't wait to finally be able to indulge in that luxury again—once his blasted cast was removed. She'd made a point to tell him she had expected, at most, something along the lines of a metal hip bath, and he'd made a mental note to tell her the saga of the tub's journey from Chicago.

She had stayed downstairs for quite a while. In fact, he had drifted off to sleep and hadn't heard her footfalls come back up the steps. It gave him a good feeling, though, to know that his home contained an item that she thoroughly enjoyed.

For the next few minutes, he tried to imagine what changes his new wife would wish to make to their home above his shop.

Charise spent some time tidying up the bathing room and supervising Toby as he brought in more firewood for the stove.

"That's enough for a while, Toby. Thank you," she smiled at the youth, suppressing a chuckle as she watched a blush infuse his face and neck.

"You're welcome, Miz Maynard. Anything else you need, you just say it and I'll do it. Don't matter what, I'll do it. I used to help out Miz Sharpe when her and Mister Sharpe had the tavern here—and the hotel above."

"Oh?" Charise couldn't help but ask, "You knew the previous owners well?"

"Heck yeah...I mean, sure thing, ma'am...I've lived here all my life. Everybody knew Mister and Miz Sharpe. They were good people. Shame about what happened..."

Finn hadn't yet told her how he had acquired the building or anything about the previous owners. Her curiosity simply couldn't be snuffed. "What happened to them, Toby?" she asked as they walked together from the bathing room into the large area containing Finn's shop.

"Well, it was a few years back. Mister Sharpe was helpin' unload some whiskey barrels off a shipper's wagon and the horses got spooked and jerked the wagon forward. Some of the barrels fell off and landed right on top of him, knocked him flat down, and busted him up inside somethin' awful. He never got over it. Miz Sharpe took over runnin' things, but they were gettin' older, didn't have no sons to help. Finally, he, Mister Sharpe, died and Miz Sharpe didn't want to have the place any longer. She blamed the tavern for her husband dyin', said it was dealing with the whiskey that done killed him. So, she put out the word that if anybody wanted the buildin', she'd sell out for the best offer."

"And Finn bought it."

"Yess'm. Everybody know'd he'd been savin' his money and wantin' to get his own business. He always said he hated workin' at the sawmill. He'd learned how to cut hair in the army durin' the war. He even cut some general's hair, and he wanted to open his own barbershop." Charise nodded, as Finn had told her a few stories about his army days. "He made her an offer and she took it. She left two days later on the stage bound for back east somewhere, Chicago, I think. I heard her tell Mr. Maynard she sold the buildin' to him cause she knew he was gonna use it for somethin' besides servin' liquor."

They had been slowly walking through the downstairs and reached the large, covered object in the corner. Charise's curiosity got the better of her once again. Heading toward it, she muttered, "I've just got to see what this monstrosity is."

Pulling on the tarp, a rank odor wafted out as it fell partially off to reveal a haphazard pile of saloon tables, chairs, spittoons, ashtrays, crates of empty glasses, and a pile of playing cards. "Mister Finn didn't know what to do with all this junk, so he just shoved it all in the corner and covered it up. Said he'd deal with it later," the youth said with a wide grin, laughing when Charise wrinkled her nose at the sight and smell of some of the objects. Goodness! The spittoons had been used—and not cleaned! She shivered in disgust.

Then she shook her head with a half smile. Surely, there must be a better use for that corner other than the storage of old saloon miscellanea. She would discuss it with Finn and see if he had any ideas yet.

Just then there was a knock on the front door and Charise turned her head to see the familiar build and face of her brother-in-law through the glass. Toby hastened over and unlocked the bolt.

Sam's face lit up and his eyes crinkled mischievously as he came in and spied Charise standing with her hands on her hips near the distasteful pile. He laughed and reached up to stroke his beard.

"I see you found out what was under there."

She looked at him, one eyebrow raised. "I did. Now I'm

wondering why it's all still here and what we can do about it."

Sam tipped back his head and released a single, loud *ha!* "You'll have to take that up with Finn."

She gave a decisive nod. "I intend to."

"How is he this morning? He still sleeping?" Sam asked teasingly. She shot him an embarrassed look, knowing he probably thought they had...gotten to know one another *carnally* during the night.

"No, he's up. I think he's out on the back porch, grumbling about being housebound."

Her burly proxy husband set his hands on his hips, his expression sobering as he considered her words. "You know...I've teased him about those steps and all, but...I could have you a staircase built in two shakes of a lamb's tail. Would you like that?"

Charise's heart thumped in gratitude at her generous brother-in-law's offer and she stepped close to him. Laying one hand on his arm, she gushed, "Oh Sam! That would be wonderful! It would help not only Finn, but me too, in so many ways. Would you really do that for us?"

Sam chuckled at her enthusiasm and patted her hand as he inclined his head affirmatively. "You betcha. I've got enough scrap lumber at the mill to build steps for half the houses in town. I'll make a few calculations and start on it in the morning, all right?"

Charise smiled and reached up on tiptoe to bestow a kiss to his beard-roughened cheek.

"Thank you, Sam. What would we ever do without you? I'm sure Finn will be as thrilled as I am."

Chapter 7

The new couple's second evening together went much like their first. Charise had spent the day finding places for the rest of her clothing and personal items, making lunch and supper for the two of them, and enduring a visit from the erstwhile Elvira. Quite early in the evening, Charise found herself bone weary, and realized the travel fatigue had finally won out over the excitement of getting used to her new home.

By the time the sun had slipped behind the top of the building next door, Charise felt as if she was going dim as well and could barely keep her eyes open. It was all she could do amidst nearly non-stop yawns to get Finn settled on the settee for the night, groggily shed her clothes, don her nightgown, and fall into bed—not stirring until the rising sun shown through the hall window and into the open bedroom door.

She rolled over in the big bed and stretched leisurely, feeling refreshed and clear headed.

Climbing out of bed, she washed herself awake at the dry sink on the stand in the corner, dressed in a fresh skirt and blouse, and made her way outside to make use of the outdoor facilities. Slipping back inside and climbing the interior steps, she peeked in to see that Finn was already stirring, so she hastened to get the fire going in the cook stove and started breakfast.

Finn had told her his favorite breakfast was French toast with honey and blackberry preserves, with crisp bacon on the side. Glad she had baked two loaves of bread the day before, she was anxious to make the dish for him using her friend Beth's recipe. *Oh...I hope we have cinnamon...*

It wasn't long before she heard a splash of water from the extra dry sink she had found in one of the storage rooms and had asked Toby to place in the parlor for Finn to use. Right on time, as she was frying the toast, she heard him thumping into the room behind her.

Her back to him as she worked at the stove, she smiled and called over her shoulder, "Good morning."

"Morning, sweetheart! Sure smells good in here. You making what I think you're making?" he asked. She heard the grin in his voice and nodded.

"Your favorite, to celebrate our second morning as husband and wife."

"Woman, you're gonna spoil me," he chuckled.

"That's the plan," she laughed as she finished his slices, placed them on a warmed plate, turned, and was suitably impressed that he was already seated and waiting.

"You're getting around quite efficiently with your crutches now," she observed as she set the plate in front of him and poured coffee in his cup. He commented that he figured he had finally found his center of balance—once the house had settled down with less...*stress*. She shook her head at him, but couldn't help a soft giggle, as she knew to what—or *whom*—he was referring.

Returning to the stove, she dipped and began to fry her own servings of the scrumptious dish.

Finn waited until she was seated before starting to eat and reached for her hand to say a quick blessing over the meal. Then, as he called her his treasure, Charise grinned.

Digging in, he moaned in delight. "Honey, these are amazing. They taste even better than Ma used to make. What do you use that's different?"

She sent him a grin and tilted her chin coquettishly. "My secret recipe. Or rather, it came from Beth Ann's grandmother, but it's still secret. I had to swear on my life not to share it," she giggled again, thoroughly pleased at his reaction.

He smiled back, his eyes sparkling with joy. "Well, whatever is in there, it sure is good."

They ate in silence for a few minutes, and then he said, "Beth Ann...that was your roommate, right?"

"Yes...and I surely miss her," she answered faintly, thinking of her best friend's teasing laughter and undying friendship. "We met at Fessenden & Stewart. She worked at the perfume counter on the first floor and I worked back in the alterations department." She met his eye and he nodded, remembering that she'd told him about her work in her letters. "We became fast friends the first day I was there," she explained, remembering those first unsure days; they had both been so young. "She was two years older than me, and seemed so accomplished and self-assured." She took another bite and glanced his way. "I don't remember if I told you, but from the age of ten Beth had been raised in an orphanage. Once you reach eighteen, they boot you out and you're on your own. She'd only been working a month when I started."

He gave a nod as he munched on a piece of crispy bacon. She continued, "Her eighteenth birthday came and she needed to find a place to live, so she asked me if I'd go in halves with her on a small apartment, and I said yes. Well, to call it an apartment is being generous—it was actually just one big room that we divided into different areas. We even shared a bed. Oh, and by the way," she added, a mischievous glint in her eye as she pointed her fork at him. "It's because of Beth Ann that I'm even here. It was *her* idea for me to check out the matrimonial advertisements after...well, after

Ethan did what he did—and she even borrowed newspapers from our elderly gentleman neighbor across the hall."

He sent her a wide grin. "I'll have to write her a thank you letter," he quipped and she giggled. Then, mockingly he added, "Sounds like she wanted the room all to herself."

"Oh no, that wasn't it. She won't be living there too much longer, herself. Her long-time beau, Stanley, no doubt will be asking for her hand soon. No, she just...she knew I wanted to get a fresh start...go somewhere new...away from...well, certain people."

He took another big bite, chewing thoughtfully before casting a glance at her. "Ethan...that's your ex-fiancé, the no-good that Sam knocked on his...*caboose*, right?"

Remembering that thoroughly entertaining incident, Charise pressed two fingers to her lips as she swallowed her bite of food and chuckled. "Yes, he is, and oh, Finn, I enjoyed every moment of that, believe me! Sam was amazing!"

Finn smiled back, but after a heartbeat, his eyes dimmed just a mite and he cleared his throat, murmuring, "Yeah, I can imagine. Good old Sam...if I could have been there, I'd have done more than just knock the blackguard on his keister. Sounds like the cad needs to be taken down a peg or two, from what you told me before."

Charise gave a nod as she pictured Ethan in his

immaculate suit, lying prostrate on the sidewalk and rubbing his jaw as he stared up at a furious Sam. "Sam stood in for you quite well. He made short work of Ethan."

They finished the rest of their breakfast in thoughtful silence.

Finn said no more, and Charise stole occasional glances at his face, but the playfulness from earlier had gone and his thoughts seemed serious...almost brooding. More than once, she wished she could read his mind and tried to think of a way to ask if something was bothering him, but nothing she thought of seemed right. Had she said something wrong earlier? As she finished up the last of her meal, she combed through their conversation in her mind, but couldn't put her finger on what the problem could be.

When Charise stood up to clear the table, idly mentioning that they were running low on a few foodstuffs, Finn quickly offered to write down items for purchase at the mercantile while she worked on the dishes and called each necessity out to him. He told her where the store, Hodge's Mercantile, was located—about five businesses down on the opposite side of the street and Charise remembered seeing it the day she arrived.

"Just tell Mr. Hodge to put everything on my account," Finn instructed, adding, "You can get some fancy doodads for the house if you want...you know, like curtains, or rag rugs, stuff like that..."

Charise finished the dishes and then came to stand at his side to peruse the list and see if she could think of anything else they needed.

He looked up at her, his eyes sparkling with affection and her heart jumped when he reached up and caressed her cheek with the backs of his fingers. His touch once again made her heart pound as tingles zipped up and down her body. Oh, how just his mere touch affected her! She leaned into his caress, her eyes locked with his as she whispered, "Thank you, Finn. You're such a wonderful husband..."

His eyes shifted to her lips and back to search her eyes as if for permission. "Charise...you're so beautiful..." he responded as his hand slowly slid around to the back of her head and he gently urged her closer. She complied without hesitation, her eyes drifting shut at the first touch of his lips to hers.

Oh my stars! She gasped lightly as tiny lights seemed to explode behind her eyelids and she melted into his kiss. He grasped her around the waist, turning her to perch on his good leg and their arms seemed to naturally wrap around one another as Finn promptly deepened the kiss.

Charise had never been kissed like this. No man she courted, nor even her ex-fiancé, had ever kissed her with such passion—and she found she liked it, instantly wanting more. At that moment, she had no doubt she and her husband were well on their way to falling in love—if their mutual attraction and this fiery kiss were any indication.

Finn moaned low in his throat and slanted his mouth across hers to glean the sweetness inside. She slipped her hands up to thread her fingers into his hair and opened to him fully...just as they both heard the sound of a handsaw being pulled through wood, coming from somewhere nearby.

She barely heard it, so intent was she on enjoying the taste and feel of her husband's tongue interacting with hers—but Finn seemed to come to himself and turned his head, breaking their kiss as he gazed toward the back door and mumbled, "What the *heck* is *that*?"

Floating down from the mountaintop of their first passionate kiss, Charise idly looked over her shoulder and listened, and then smiled as she realized what they were hearing.

"Oh, that's just Sam. I forgot to tell you, he's building us a back staircase today."

"He's *what?*" Her suddenly irate husband demanded, turning angry sapphire eyes her way. She had not expected such a response. Hadn't dreamed of it.

Oh goodness. What have I done?

"Get up, get up," Finn urged, boosting Charise up off his lap so quickly she nearly lost her balance. He then reached for his crutches as the noise of the saw seemed to get louder and louder, the rasping sound abrading his nerves. For some reason, he wasn't taking time to analyze the situation and his temper exploded like coal oil flung on a bonfire as he struggled to his good foot and lurched to the back door... *on a mission.*

"Finn! My goodness, what's wrong?" Charise squeaked from somewhere behind him. He could hear her hurrying to catch up. "It's *Sam.*" She reiterated. "He offered yesterday when he was here. I thought you'd be thrilled..." she tried to reason with him as he stubbornly ignored her. Reaching the door, he wrenched it open.

"He didn't *ask* me, that's what's wrong," he muttered as he maneuvered through the door, his crutches banging into the doorjamb on either side. *Dang that brother of mine, coming over here and taking over, like I'm not even here. First, he marries my intended because I'm laid up like an invalid, then he plays the dashing hero and punches the daylights out of her rude ex-fiancé, and now this. I've had it.* His pride had taken all it could stand. All of the pent up frustration of the last two weeks came to a head and completely ignoring how ridiculous his argument would seem, he groused, "You don't just take on a project at another man's house like that without clearin' it with the *man*! Building steps on my place is *my* job. Not *his*."

"B...but..." she sputtered as they emerged together onto the wood surface of the porch. Simmering, he crutched his way to the railing and glared down, seeing the top of his brother's head as he bent over the saw.

"Hey!" Finn barked. "What'dya think you're *doin'?*"

Finn noticed Charise, eyes rounded as she peeked over the railing just as Sam looked up, saw her and sent her a wave, before he turned his attention back to him. The steam inside Finn rose another ten degrees as he saw the mirth in his brother's eyes. If there was one thing that could always ratchet up his rage it was his brother laughing or making fun of his fury.

"What's it look like I'm doin', Finny? I'm buildin' you a staircase—the staircase *you* should have built when you tore the other one down," he stated matter-of-factly. Then switching his gaze to Charise again, he grinned and tipped an invisible hat to her, calling up, "Top of the morning to you, sunshine."

Charise opened her mouth to answer, but Finn, irrationally raging, flung up a hand to cut her off, then pointed a finger down at Sam. "She's not *your* sunshine. She's *my* wife, not *yours,* you got that? That proxy marriage doesn't mean she belongs to you. She belongs to *ME*! And this *house* don't belong to you *either!* You can't just come waltzing over here and put up a staircase any old time you feel like it! You—"

"Phineas Oliver!" his wife's screech interrupted his tirade. He jerked to a stop, and turned to stare at her, shocked speechless at her outburst. Through his haze of anger, he saw that her mouth had fallen open and she'd turned to gape at him like he was a stranger who had taken over the body of her sweet tempered, wonderful new husband. *Where had that thought come from?* Finn tried to shove it away as his new wife lit into him like old Mrs. Travis had that time he'd stolen a whole blackberry pie right off her windowsill.

"How *dare* you speak to Sam like that!" Charise yelled. "What in the world are you so angry about...and why are you saying such things to your own *brother*?" Although rapidly losing the vigor of his anger like a boiling pot taken off the fire, Finn opened his mouth to defend himself, but she barreled on, "Sam's been nothing but wonderful to us both—and you well know it!" She stopped and swallowed hard, obviously trying to rein in her own temper.

"Th...that's beside the point," Finn stuttered in retort, but she shook her head in disgust and continued, "I'm ashamed of you, Finn Maynard, and right now, I feel like I don't know you at all. You ought to be ashamed of *yourself*, talking to your brother like that. You ought to try showing a little *gratitude*. Sam's taking time out from his own business to come over here and help us."

She paused, her chest heaving, which in his opinion made her look alluring as all get out. Her words had made him feel lower than a dung beetle; even as part of his brain managed to register that she looked amazingly fetching all riled up like she was. Those brown eyes of hers were sparklingly animated, her face was pink with exertion, and that kissable mouth was clamped shut in frustration. Abstractly, he wanted to grab her and kiss her all over again, but before he could move, she brought up a shaking hand and pointed at him, her finger nearly touching his nose as she added, "You need to apologize, Mr. Maynard."

He swallowed and watched as she glanced over the rail at an equally shocked Sam, and called, "I'm going to the mercantile. I'll see you later, Sam," then she turned on her heel and stomped to the door. Finn couldn't take his eyes from the amazing creature he had married as she whirled around, skirts swirling and dark braid swinging, her whole body still shaking with emotion as she reiterated, "*Apologize.*"

Then she went through the door and slammed it behind her, rattling the glass panes in the process.

Sam reacted with chuckling from down below. "Whew doggies, now you went and done it."

Finn shut his mouth, which had fallen open during his wife's tirade. *Dang, she sure got mad. All I said was...was...*

his thoughts stopped, suddenly unable to remember why he'd even gotten so angry, or what he had said to his brother during his few minutes of mindless rage. He was sure, however, that it hadn't been as bad as some of their scraps had been growing up. Sam had said worse to him in the past. Heck, during some of their brawls, they had ended up coming to blows, one time even rolling around in the mud, bellowing and howling like two rabid bears! But, they always made up and let bygones be bygones. That's the way of brothers...

He clutched the rail with both hands and looked down at his amused sibling, who stood staring up at him, chortling and scratching his head.

"My my, that little gal's got a temper. I think you've done met your match, Finny boy. She gone off at you like that before?" Sam couldn't seem to quit his chuckling.

Finn shook his head. "Nope. We've been getting along great. Matter of fact, we were just..." he paused, not necessarily wishing to share with his wisecracking brother about his and Charise's first magnificent, earth-shattering kiss. He knew Sam would get a big kick out of having interrupted the momentous event and Finn would probably never hear the end of it. He clamped his mouth shut.

Sam called up, "Why *did* you light into me like that, anyway?"

Finn's eyes slipped closed as he shook his head and chuckled. "Heck if I know. I guess..." he opened his eyes and met his brother's patient stare. He knew Sam understood him—probably better than he understood *himself.*

Suddenly, he did feel the shame his wife had heaped on him and he looked down at the aggravating cast on his leg and then back at his brother with a crooked half grin. "Aww horse feathers, Sam. I'm so cotton pickin' tired of being laid up with this stupid cast, not able to be a man, a husband, a barber, or even a *brother*, I just went a little crazy there, I guess." Sam grinned up at him, obviously enjoying his discomfort. Deciding to take his lumps like a man, Finn went on, "I guess...I guess I've felt a bit jealous of...well, dang it, of you and Charise. *There, I said* it. It's kinda seemed like you two have a special relationship that don't have anything to do with *me*, and I keep thinking about those vows you spoke with each other and...well, *con sarnit,"* he paused and rifled one hand back through his hair. "You're all big and burley and strong, and a *whole man*, while I'm stuck up here, can't even walk, can't work, can't go anywhere, can't—"

"Now just hold on one biscuit eatin' minute. You keep this up, you're gonna get *me* riled." Sam warned, albeit gently. He took a deep breath and ran his hand down his bushy face. Looking back up at Finn, he went on, "Number one, you're a *whole man* same as me. Just cause you temporarily got a busted leg don't make you less of a man.

Number two, I can tell by the way Charise already looks at you, watches you, hangs on every word you say, that *you're* already special in her heart—more special than *I* can ever be. She's already got feelings for ya; it's as plain as the nose on her face. Number three, those *vows* you're so worried about—that judge worded 'em so that she was pledging to love, honor and *obey YOU*. He made sure to use your name, not mine. And you haven't asked, but I didn't kiss her on the mouth when he gave the word, just like I promised I wouldn't. I kissed her cheek—and I told her why."

Finn watched as Sam tossed the saw down and placed his hands on his hips, staring up at him. "And as for you being stuck up there—you jughead—that's why I'm over here at the crack of dawn planning on working all day and probably all of tomorrow too, building you an escape route so you won't be *stuck up there* anymore." Then as if a realization just occurred to him, he dropped his hands to his sides and sheepishly admitted, "But I guess I did kind of jump into the thick of things, though, huh?"

All of the tension between the brothers seemed to evaporate like dew in the morning sun and they both started to chuckle, and then guffaw. Finn bent over the rail laughing as Sam gleefully slapped his own thigh.

"I'm sorry." "I apologize." They said in unison.

Sam peered up at Finn one more time and said, "Lemme

come up there and we'll sit together at the kitchen table and draw up some plans for this here staircase. How's that sound?"

"Sounds like a plan, brother. I'll meet you inside. I think there's some coffee left from breakfast."

Once the door banged shut behind her, Charise curled her hands into fists and stomped her foot in a mini fit. "*Oooooo that man!*" She hadn't felt that angry in such a long time, she couldn't remember when. *And this on the heels of that earth-moving, grab-a-bucket-and-douse-the-fire kiss!*

Her emotions felt twisted and confused toward her new husband.

Finn's accusations had been completely unreasonable toward Sam, whom she already loved like a brother, and the entirety had ignited a fierce loyalty within Charise. Also, Finn's blustering about her *belonging* to him and not Sam had set her teeth on edge, chiefly because he'd said it as if she weren't standing there—as if she had needed defending *from* Sam. Goodness, where had all *that* come from?

What a way to start a morning...not to mention a marriage.

Still fuming, and at present wishing to be as far from Finn as she could get, she grabbed his list off the table, marched to the bedroom, and snatched up her reticule. Stomping down the hall and the steps, she muttered the entire way about stubborn, stupid, grouchy husbands. She exited the front door of the building with a firm bang, though not quite a slam, and set off marching down the boardwalk.

Thankfully, by the time she crossed the threshold of the mercantile, a good bit of her anger had dissipated. She stepped inside and took in a deep, cleansing breath, reveling in all of the different smells and aromas in the large, well-stocked general store. Animal feed, lamp oil, yard goods, and salted meat—the array was quite impressive. Allowing her eyes to adjust to the dimmer light, she looked around the fairly large space, her list held tightly in one hand.

A man came through a door in the back wall and walked toward her as he tied the strings of a white, merchant's apron behind his back, a friendly smile wreathing his wrinkled face. Charise noticed he had smooth, silver hair that was attractively combed and he had tied the apron folded over at his belt so that his crisp, white shirt, striped gray and white vest and black string tie were visible. *My what a sharp-dressed man—even in a shopkeeper's apron.*

"Good morning there, missy," he greeted and she found herself smiling at his easy personality. "I'm Sebastian Hodge. I own this here establishment."

She gave a nod and answered, "Good morning."

"You're Finny's new wife, ain't ya," he stated, giving her the once-over with a decisive nod. "Big Sam told me how pretty you are, and he was sure right."

Charise felt her face heat under the compliment and his observant gaze as she murmured, "Why...thank you."

"How's young Finn doin'? Ain't seen him since he had his accident. Darn shame, that was."

"Oh, he's doing better. Learning to navigate with his crutches," she answered, working to tamp down the embers of her earlier upset.

He looked down at the paper in her hand. "That your list?"

She started and cleared her throat as she handed it over. "Oh! Yes, thank you. We need quite a few things. I'm afraid Finn's pantry was barely stocked with only the most basic of essentials."

The older man tipped back his head and laughed. "Typical bachelor. I think he usually took his meals at the Blue Bird...that's the café over on 1st Street," he clarified as he moved to a shelf on the wall to begin filling her order. "I'll get these things together for you in no time—I imagine you want to get back to him right fast."

Charise opened her mouth and said the first thing that popped into her mind. "Oh no, really. Take your time. I'm in no hurry." At his somewhat surprised glance, her face flushed at her blunt reply and she turned to begin perusing the store. She'd made it all the way around the walls and examined most of the center tables, barrels, and display shelves when the bell over the door jingled and a man in a long, black frock coat along with a woman in an attractive rust colored dress came in, followed closely by the familiar face—and voice—of Elvira Davis.

Good heavens, her again? Her conscience instantly pinched at her uncharitable thought and she winced. *Okay, time to scrape up some Christian charity, Charise Olivia, and smile at the woman. Like you admonished your husband just minutes ago, you need to show a little gratitude...after all, the woman went out of her way to take care of Finn before you got here. Try to ignore the fact that her incessant jabber-mouthing drives you to distraction, sets your teeth on edge, and makes you want to run away screaming...*

Forcing a smile at the three newcomers, Charise murmured, "Hello, Elvira," before raising her eyebrows to the couple.

Elvira jumped right in, of course. "Morning, Charise! Why, how's our patient this morning? I'll bet he's grouchy, just like always, huh? That man just seems to get grumpier by the day. Have you met Reverend McKnight and his lovely wife, Rachael? Reverend, Rachael, this here is Finn Maynard's new proxy mail-order-bride, Charise. Reverend

McKnight is the pastor of the First Baptist Church down at the other end of Main, don't you know. He's been pastor there for nigh on three years, now, ain't that right, Reverend? And Rachael—"

"Pleased to make your acquaintance, Mrs. Maynard," the man in the black coat blessedly interrupted the barrage of words and stepped forward, holding his hand out. "The wife and I were just saying that we needed to pay you and Finn a call, but we were giving you a few days to settle in."

"Nice to meet you both," Charise shook their hands, breathing a bit easier as Elvira made a beeline for the back of the store where a woman with salt and pepper hair wearing a full storekeeper's white apron over a plaid work dress was just coming through a doorway. "Miz Hodge! I just have to tell you something!"

Charise turned back to the Reverend and his wife, the three of them exchanging looks that let each of them know they were of one accord.

Reverend McKnight smiled kindly and glanced at his wife with knowing amusement before engaging Charise's eyes again. "Miss Elvira is one of Brownville's more...shall we say...*loquacious* citizens."

Stifling a chuckle while being pleasantly impressed that the kind man of God had found a nice way of saying the obnoxious woman was unreserved...chatty...gossipy...gabby...windy...or downright motor mouthed, Charise agreed, "Yes, she certainly is that."

The three laughed together softly, the ice effectively broken.

"Well, how do you think you're going to like living in Brownville, Mrs. Maynard?" the parson's wife asked warmly.

"Oh, please call me Charise. And, I think I'm going to like it just fine. In some ways it is quite different from where I'm from, of course...but in other ways I see similarities."

"And where *are* you from, Charise?"

"Louisville, Kentucky."

"Ahh, a beautiful city, right on the Ohio. I spent some time there during the war," Reverend McKnight put in with a pleasant smile.

"Really? How interesting," Charise replied, searching his amiable gaze.

"I was a chaplain for the union army during the war and was stationed in Louisville for a short time," he answered her unspoken question.

"What a wonderful coincidence," Charise was delighted, already feeling a connection with the kind couple.

"Yes, happily so," he charmingly agreed. "But now, if

you'll excuse me, ladies, I don't mean to rush off, but I'm afraid that I need to consult with Sebastian about a matter. Very nice to meet you, Charise. We look forward to having you join us for worship on Sunday...unless you'd rather wait for Phineas to be able to accompany you, in which case, we'll see you as soon as you can."

"Yes, thank you," Charise smiled as the Reverend tipped his hat, kissed his wife lovingly on the cheek, and set off across the store to where Mr. Hodge was putting several jugs of lamp oil into a box for Charise.

Mrs. McKnight turned back just as Charise was unexpectedly hit with a pang of conscience at how she had yelled at her husband and stormed off out of the house, angry as a wet hen. Now, the whole thing seemed almost silly.

Beaming demurely, the woman placed a hand on Charise's arm. When Charise peered into her eyes, she saw within their wise gaze a lady who had been married a long time and was a kind, caring person.

"Is everything all right, dear?"

Charise felt herself blush once again and looked down at her fingers that had suddenly begun twisting the strings of her reticule. "Oh...I..." she paused and then looked into the woman's understanding eyes. For some reason, she heard herself blurt, "I'm afraid I've only been here two days and Finn and I have already had our first fight—and oh my, was it a barn burner."

To her surprise, Rachael McKnight tipped back her head and let out a delightful laugh. "Oh my dear, believe it or not, that is a good sign."

Charise's brow furrowed. She had thought her and Finn's exchange that morning anything but good.

"I beg your pardon?"

The older woman slipped an arm around Charise and gave her a sideways squeeze. "My wise old granny used to say that any couple that doesn't have a tiff once in a while has a dull, boring marriage. She called it having a good old-fashioned 'rhubarb'. It sounds like you and our dear Finn are off to a rousing start—and your marriage will be anything but dull!"

Charise tried to respond in the affirmative, but right then, she could think of better ways to keep her and Finn's marriage interesting.

CHAPTER 8

Charise walked slowly and thoughtfully down the boardwalk, dreading the moment when she would see her husband again.

Was he still angry? In truth, did he have a bad temper that she would have to watch out for or try to placate throughout their entire marriage? Would this put a permanent chink in their relationship?

Now that she had calmed down, she was a bit surprised at herself that she had figuratively jumped on her new husband with both feet as she had and bawled him out—in front of his brother, no less. She had no doubt shamed him, and as Rachael had warned, a woman needs to be careful not to shame her husband and hurt his pride, especially in front of another man. Rachael had also astutely surmised that Finn had developed jealous feelings and they had erupted in a rather volcanic manner. The whole thing had happened so fast; she hadn't taken the time to think it through. She had just reacted, jumping to Sam's defense.

Mrs. McKnight had been wonderful; a godsend, actually. She had invited Charise to step outside of the mercantile to speak privately, and they had strolled together down the wide, dirt street and settled onto a bench, built around the base of a huge oak that was situated on the bluff overlooking the river. Charise had found herself unreservedly confiding to the kind woman who was so easy to talk with and such an obliging listener. More than that, she had been able to give Charise some much-needed marital advice.

There had been no pattern that Charise could follow in order to be a good wife, and no one had ever provided guidance on what, indeed, made a good marriage. Having lost her mother at a young age, and even before that, her mother had not had the time to council her young daughter on the ways of men and marriage—she had been far too busy going out and having fun. For her mother, life had been all about parties, the latest fashions, and what new bauble she could talk her husband into buying for her next. For the most part, Charise and her brothers had been left to the care of a very strict, all business housekeeper and nanny.

But God knows our needs and He had now sent a mentor into Charise's life. After her heartfelt talk with Rachael, Charise now felt she had some tools with which to go about this thing called marriage.

But first, she needed to know something about her husband that only an outsider would be truthful about.

Now, she turned to Toby, who was pushing a wheeled cart down the boardwalk at her side, laden with her purchases.

"Toby...may I ask you a question?"

His eyes rounded and he glanced at her as he maneuvered the cart along, narrowly avoiding a pole holding up the porch in front of the bank. "Sure, Miz Maynard. You can ask me anything."

Charise breathed in deeply, steadying her resolve. If she had married a hot-tempered man, so be it. She would cope. Still, forewarned is forearmed, her father used to say.

"Does Finn...does Finn normally have a bad temper?"

Toby seemed to mull the question over before answering. Finally, with a small shrug, he answered, "Not really, ma'am. I mean, he gets mad sometimes, sure, like everybody else. But, I've never seen him hit nobody, or be violent like some men get—especially when they've had too much to drink over at the Lucky Buck or the Whistle Stop. Heck, he didn't even get mad at me when I caused his leg to get busted!"

Relieved on that score, Charise smiled at the young man. "I'm relieved to hear that. Thank you, Toby."

All too soon, they were at the door of the building and there was nothing for it but to go inside. Bolstering her determination, she pushed open the door and entered, then held it wide for Toby to pass with her purchases.

Taking hold of a bag, each of flour and sugar, she headed up the steep, narrow, winding steps, carefully holding her skirt out of the way and silently blessing Sam for his willingness to build them a real staircase. Arriving at the landing, she took a deep, fortifying breath and marched forward, heading for the kitchen. As she passed the bedroom and parlor she glanced in, but Finn wasn't in either room, nor was he in the kitchen.

On the table, however, were two coffee cups, a stub of a pencil, and several crumpled sheets of paper. She looked toward the porch door. *He must have gone back out on the porch...did he send Sam home?*

Charise turned as Toby came in carrying a large box, and she proceeded to begin the process of finding places to stash the items she had purchased at the store. Perhaps she could talk Finn into building her a small pantry in the corner later...

She took her time, stalling before seeking her husband out. She knew she had to face him, but she needed the time to gather her nerve.

Finally, when everything was put away and the kitchen tidied, she sent Toby home for the day with a thank you for his invaluable help, and several muffins that had been left over from yesterday's baking.

Approaching the back door, Charise smoothed her hair and ran her hands down her blouse and skirt to relieve them of wrinkles, then reached out for the knob—and stopped. Through the thick wooden door, she could hear Finn laughing out on the porch. *He's laughing! Well, that's a relief.*

Moistening her lips, she turned the handle and opened the door to a delightful and unexpected image of brotherly camaraderie.

Finn and Sam were both on the porch. Finn was perched with his casted leg propped up—on a pillow, no less—and two impromptu saw horses in front of him. He was hard at work with a small hand saw, cutting notches in what would be wooden treads for the new steps. Covered in sawdust and wood shavings, he looked happy as a clam, with Sam in much the same condition and activity sitting close by.

Blissfully industrious, they both looked over when she opened the door.

As her eyes met her husband's, he sent her a most welcome grin and held up the board he had been working on as both men called, "Hey Charise!" Finn added, "Wait 'till you see what we're building!"

*What **we're** building...how amazing those three little words sound.* She stepped out onto the porch, switched her gaze to Sam, who had a smile so big plastered to his face even his beard seemed to be grinning, and back to her husband.

"Look how much we've got done for the new staircase," Finn said, indicating a good-sized pile of precisely cut stair treads that were about four feet in length.

"Finn and I worked out a design for it that we hope you're gonna love," Sam put in, motioning her over so that she could see a paper drawing they had tacked to the porch rail. "The old steps went straight out and took up a lot of room from the space out back, so Finn came up with a better way." The porch extended the full width of the building, and they had drawn the landing for the new steps to drop down from the porch on the far right end with an immediate ninety-degree angle and nice, wide steps going straight down to the ground, anchored to the porch supports. *No curves.* She couldn't suppress a smile at that, knowing Finn had probably insisted upon it. There were full handrails drawn on both sides, complete with balusters.

"It's a lovely design. Looks very sturdy," she complimented.

"Finn had saved all of the usable balusters when he tore down the big front staircase, so if we use those, we should have it finished by the weekend," Sam explained.

"And then later on, we thought we'd add a roof over the porch, replace some of the warped boards...maybe even screen it in. Would you like that, Charise?" Finn asked, catching her eye again. The look on his face was so hopeful and eager as a little boy, as if her answer meant the world to him. He was so different from the angry man she had left out here hours ago.

"That sounds wonderful, Finn..." Charise began, trying to take it all in. Finn laid aside the tread he was working on and held out his hand to her. She immediately crossed the space between them and took it. His hand already seemed familiar—warm and slightly calloused—as they had joined hands to say grace many times.

He tugged her close to his side and sat looking up at her, her hand cradled between his own hand and his chest. Sam chivalrously got up and went in the house to give them a bit of privacy.

When the door closed, Finn cleared his throat and moistened his lips and she knew he was probably as nervous as she was. That knowledge helped her relax a bit more.

"Charise, I need to apologize to you. This morning, I acted like a horse's a—" he paused and altered his word, "hind-end. I'm sorry I got so mad at Sam—and lit into him in front of you like that. Truth is..." he paused, his eyes sparkling as he gazed up at her, "truth is, I was feelin' useless and downright jealous. But, Sam straightened me out—like only that big brother of mine can do," he added with a chuckle. "I know we don't know each other real well yet, you and I...but, I want you to know that the Finn Maynard you witnessed this morning ain't the real me. Ask anybody—I'm usually a pretty happy go lucky kind of guy. And honey...I don't want you to ever feel like you can't be around me."

He paused as he watched her eyes begin to tear up, his words warming her heart and answering so many questions and concerns she'd nursed all morning long. Indeed, nursed them until they had grown like weeds in a vegetable patch. Tenderly, he continued, "I'm glad you stood up to me and set me straight, sweetheart. You just keep on settin' me straight for the rest of our lives, and we'll have us a good life together. All right?"

Enormously relieved and fighting a lump of emotion in her throat, Charise managed a smile and answered thickly, "All right, Finn."

"Do you forgive me, darlin'?"

At that, she laughed softly and lowered herself down onto his good leg, wrapping her arms around his neck. "Yes, my husband. I forgive you. And to prove that," she added, peering around jestingly in the guise of making sure they were alone. "I'd like to get back to what we were doing before we were so rudely interrupted this morning—how 'bout you?"

Finn grinned from ear to ear and then tipped back his head and hooted in glee. "Yes, ma'am, I was hopin' you'd say that."

With one more relieved look into one another's eyes, each knowing they had weathered their first storm and come out better for it, Finn leaned forward and captured her lips.

Great day in the morning, their second kiss was even better than the first!

Two weeks later...

Sitting at her new desk that Finn had asked Sam and Toby to carry up for her and placed by one of the large windows in the front room, Charise tapped the end of her pen against her lips and contemplated what else to tell her friend back home. It was the first time she had taken the time to write, so she wanted to fill Beth in on everything that had happened in the interim.

Having lost her train of thought when the sound of wagon chains on the street below had stolen her attention, she gathered up the freshly inked sheets of paper to read over what she had written thus far.

Dearest Beth,

Greetings from Brownville, Nebraska!

Did I thank you, dear friend, for standing up with me at my proxy wedding and seeing Sam and me off when we boarded the train? If I was negligent, then I'm thanking you now.

Oh Beth, so much has happened in the past two weeks, I hardly know how to get it all down on paper. First, I know you're dying to know about Finn, so I will tell you—he is wonderful. His leg in that enormous cast—and oh my word, Beth, you would not believe how big and heavy it is—has healed completely now and the doctor has said he will remove it in the morning. I think I'm almost as anxious as Finn for that to happen...well, that might be a bit of an exaggeration.

Finn Maynard is even more handsome than his portrait suggested. He's warm, generous, romantic and affectionate, and so far he has been a darling husband. Well...except for one incident. We laugh about it now. Seems he had let his imagination run wild and had formed a jealousy toward Sam regarding me. Can you imagine? Sam—he's already more of a big brother to me than my own ever were and I know he feels I am more like a sister to him as well. But my sweet Finn...well, let's just say, it was a bump in the road, but we got over it and the rest of the path has been smooth traveling thus far. Both my husband and my brother-in-law are incessant teasers, however, and they keep me on my toes.

I wish you could see our home, Beth. We live in a hotel!

I'm joking, partly. The building Finn owns and in which he has his shop has a second floor that used to be the town's first hotel. The downstairs had been a tavern called the Lone Tree Saloon. You read that right, a saloon—complete with one of the longest, most ornate bars you could ever imagine. Finn had just been storing crates on it. It still has the whiskey glasses and other things below it—everything except liquor, Finn got rid of all of that the first thing, and I'm so very glad he's not a drinking man. We have a few ideas for the bar area, but so far we haven't decided.

The top floor, where we make our home, is not overly large; although twenty feet by seventy feet is much larger than average homes and certainly larger than the one room you and I shared for all those years. We have a good sized kitchen on the back end, a parlor, our bedroom, a center hallway, two rooms we are saving for guests or whoever may come along in the future, and a large room at the front that I have turned into my sewing and craft room. Plus, I can have friends over for tea and sweet cakes in here if I want.

Charise paused in her reading as she smiled at that last sentence, and looked out the window to see one of her new friends—Dorothea—strolling down the street on her husband's arm. Dorothea and Dave had a wonderful marriage, and Charise counted herself blessed to have Dottie, as everyone called her, as a much welcomed and dear friend. Watching Dottie laugh at something her husband said, Charise smiled a bit wider and then chuckled and shook her head, remembering when her sweet friend had explained her odd comment that first evening regarding her knowing the way up to Finn's quarters. It seemed that when Dottie had first come to town, she had stayed at the hotel as a guest. Oh, how the imagination can conjure up things that are so far from the truth!

Looking back to the papers in her hand, she turned to the next page and continued reading.

After the first few days, I settled in and it didn't take me long to feel comfortable here. Brownville is a quiet little town, but it is steadily growing. It has two brickyards and two sawmills, a large school building big enough for primary and secondary students, two banks, two druggists, several mercantile stores, three churches—including a Baptist church, a Lutheran church, and a Catholic parish. It also has ten saloons! When I first found that out, I admit I was a bit shocked, but several of those are what Finn calls a "hole in the wall" and are merely ramshackle little huts down at the wharf. The most popular tavern is called the Lucky Buck. I still haven't found out why Sam and Finn give one another odd looks anytime someone mentions that infamous establishment.

Remember Sam regaling us with stories about the impossibly narrow staircase to Finn's quarters and how it had made him a virtual prisoner? Well, my wonderful brother-in-law (with Finn helping as much as he could) crafted us the most sturdy, well-built set of steps any girl could ask for, descending down from our back porch off the kitchen. From the day they were finished, Finn was able to negotiate his way down them with his crutches and was freed of his cage! He was so excited; he insisted the three of us go out to eat at one of the eateries in town; a place one street over called the Blue Bird Café that has the most delicious food. Although he was fatigued when we got home, it was the happiest I had seen him since my arrival. Oh that reminds me...some day I'll have to tell you the story of the first time Finn and I saw one another face to face.

Since the next day after the steps were finished, Finn has been back at work in his barbershop, much relieved to be working again. The poor dear, it was very hard on him to be stuck up here with practically nothing to do, feeling useless, as he put it. Although there is another barbershop in town, Finn has regular, loyal customers who did not desert him while he was incapacitated—and some of those are colorful, to say the least. However, that meant that his first few days back on the job were quite busy. I even helped shave several scruffy faces while Finn rested his leg. That was an experience!

Did I mention that my husband is sweetly romantic? He's told me how he had planned on courting me after I had come to marry him (before the proxy idea), and he still wants *to do so. He said he's pulling out all of the stops, as he wants me to always remember and cherish our "courting" days. Truly, has there ever been a more romantic, wonderful mail-order groom?*

In a few weeks, once Finn is able to walk normally again (the doctor said his leg muscles might be weak at first), and in his words, he's able to literally sweep me off my feet, we are planning to have a ceremony for he and I to retake our vows—to one another, in church with the reverend presiding. Our friends are throwing us a celebration party afterwards—although it will be downstairs in the area Finn doesn't use as his shop! I wish you could be here standing at my side again...but at least I'll be able to wear my wedding dress this time.

Finn and I haven't been to church as a couple yet. I wanted to wait until he could escort me, since I knew it would only be a matter of a few weeks. I'm looking forward to attending this coming Sunday. I've met the Reverend McKnight and his wonderful wife. She's already a dear friend, as well as a surrogate mother figure for me.

Beth...I know I said at first that your idea of me becoming a mail-order-bride was the craziest thing ever, but...I want to tell you now—thank you. Thank you for reading the advertisements with me, and for helping me write my first letter to Finn. I've thanked the Lord for him nearly every day since the day we met. Truly, he's everything I ever wanted in a love and a husband. I hope you and Stanley find as much happiness together as Finn and I already have.

Hearing the bell over the door downstairs jingle signaling a customer and knowing Finn would be getting hungry for lunch soon, Charise smiled happily and put the finishing touches on the letter, including a promise to write more soon.

Sealing the envelope with a dab of wax, she took it with her, intending to ask Toby if he'd deliver it to the post office at the depot, and started to prepare lunch.

The removal of Finn's cast had been more of an ordeal than either of them had anticipated, but the resulting freedom was well worth the strain. Finn had immediately begun the arduous task of working out the stiffness and pain. He was a man on a mission.

Several days later, Charise was changing the sheets on the bed as the early afternoon sun lit up the room. Humming softly, she turned with a pillow tucked under her chin as she wiggled the case into place, and her husband silently appeared at the door. Starting a bit as she spotted him, with a yelp, she dropped the pillow on the bed.

"Goodness Finn! I didn't hear you come upstairs," she chuckled. "I had grown accustomed to you thumping around the house with your cast and crutches," she added with an impish grin.

"Yeah. I thank God and Doc Reeves that the blasted thing is a just a bad memory now," he grunted as he advanced into the room, his eyes a tad intense. Her heart rate began to increase as he neared and she realized this was the first time they had ever been together inside the bedroom. That realization made her skin tingle as images of the things that would happen there in the future swam before her eyes.

He stopped near to her and gently reached out, reverently clasping her arms and tugging her up against his chest. His eyes met hers for a brief moment as his head began to lower, his warm lips taking hers in a fiery kiss. Goodness, her head began to swim! The pillowcase she had been holding slipped out of her fingers as her arms rose of their own accord, her hands wrapping themselves around the nape of her husband's neck as she kissed him back with equal passion.

Since the day of their big argument, they'd indulged in quite a few lengthy kissing sessions, each one passionate and more arousing than the one before—this particular one being no exception. Charise already adored the way her husband kissed and every coherent thought flew right out of her head the moment he started.

Great Caesar's Ghost, this man can kiss!

Minutes went by before Finn began to loosen his hold on her and forced himself to take a half step back. By then, they were both breathless and Charise felt a bit wobbly in the knees.

Pressing one hand to her now mussed hair and hazily looking up into those sparkling sapphire eyes, she managed to murmur, "My stars, Finn, what was that for? Not that I'm complaining, mind you."

He let out a naughty chuckle and leaned forward until their foreheads were touching. "I closed the shop early and came up to ask if you wanted to take a picnic supper and go for a buggy ride along the river. But once I saw you here...changing the sheets on the bed where we'll soon get to know one another...totally and completely...I kinda lost my head and just had to kiss you." He bent close and captured her lips for another taste. "And I'll say one thing, honey, your kisses take my breath away." She felt her cheeks pinken as he leaned closer and whispered in her ear, his warm breath arousing an electrified flash down her body as he placed tiny kisses to her cheek and the spot below her ear, "It seems like our real weddin' night'll never get here..." he touched his lips to her earlobe and murmured, "You got no idea how anxious I am to make you mine."

She hugged him close and whispered back, "I'm anxious too, Finn. But..."

He pulled in a deep breath and gave a nod, dropping a quick kiss to the tip of her nose and stepping back. "I know.

We said we'd wait, and we're gonna wait. No matter if it ties me up in knots," he added with a snort. "So...how about that picnic?"

Charise giggled and bent to retrieve the dropped pillowcase. "As soon as I finish here." Then raising back up, she gave him a saucy grin and a wink, adding, "You wanna help change the sheets on *our* bed?"

He dropped his head back and groaned, "Woman, you're killin' me!"

She burst out laughing and tossed him the second pillowcase, which he wrangled onto the stubborn pillow amidst much good-natured grumbling.

An hour later, they were sitting together in a borrowed buggy atop a rise that overlooked a long expanse and curve of the Missouri River. They could see the landing and wharf of the town, and a steamboat that was currently docked and unloading cargo.

"Oh Finn, it's so lovely up here. The river is beautiful from this view."

"Yeah, I love this place. It's one of the places I used to go sometimes...to think...or brood," he added with a chuckle.

She nodded knowingly. "I used to go up on the top of our building and sit by myself sometimes. It had a flat roof and someone had put chairs and even a small table up there. The stars were beautiful looking up at them from the roof," she added with a soft exhale.

Finn turned and slipped his arm around her shoulders, drawing her against his side. "We both had places to go to get away. Just another thing we have in common, huh?"

"I'd say so," she sighed contentedly.

They sat in silence for a while, watching a few of the smaller boats plying the river, and then Finn turned and faced her on the buggy seat. The look in his eyes let her know he was about to make an announcement, and her heart sped up, her hands tingling when he took them in his.

He looked deep into her eyes. "Sweetheart...it's been gnawing at me that we did everything backwards. We got married first, then we started to get to know one another, now we're courting...so, I want to tell you something." He paused and she held her breath in anticipation. "Char," he murmured, using her nickname as his eyes glinted with emotion. "My beautiful Charise, my lovely wife...I've fallen in love with you—quicker and deeper than I even dreamed I would. I want to do it right and propose proper. So—my dearest, I can't imagine life without you now...will you marry me—again—and do me the honor of speaking marriage vows with me?"

Charise had realized recently that she had fallen in love with her husband—and now her eyes filled with tears of joy, everlasting delight, and relief to know that Finn felt the same.

She sniffled dulcetly and managed a sweet smile and a nod as she answered, "Oh Finn, I love you, too...truly, deeply...madly. And yes, I'll marry you again and speak my vows while gazing into your beautiful midnight blue eyes."

He smiled devotedly and gently took hold of her left hand, slid the plain gold band off and replaced it with an elegant 18kt yellow gold engagement ring, housing five small diamonds in a row.

She caught her breath as the facets glittered in the rays of the setting sun. "Oh, Finn," she breathed. "It's splendid!"

He raised her hand to his lips for a sweet, caressing kiss. "It was my ma's. Pa said he'd asked her to marry him right before he left on a long cattle drive, and she said she would, but only if he'd buy her a nice ring for making her wait so long for him to get back. So—he did. Cost him half his pay for the drive, but he said it was worth it to see Ma's face when he put it on her."

Charise blinked moisture from her eyes and met his adoring gaze. "I'll cherish it always, Finn." She held it to her cheek for several beats, and then with a mischievous glimmer in her gaze, she announced, "I have something for you, too. I've just been waiting for the right moment to give it to you."

"Mmm, that right?" he murmured as he watched her open her reticule and rummage around inside, finally removing a smallish item rolled up in a swatch of blue velvet.

Her eyes holding his again, she reached out and grasped his hand, placing the object in his palm before waiting for him to unroll it.

Inside was a solid gold steamship wheel watch fob on a chain, with a short offshoot chain holding a miniature anchor. The wheel was inlaid with eighteen tiny diamond chips. Finn's mouth opened in surprise as he attentively examined her gift and the exquisite workmanship of each item. "This is a fine fob," he murmured, meeting her ardent gaze. "I've never seen one like it."

"It was Papa's. Mama had it made for him on the first anniversary of starting his packet company. He wore it all the time. One day, near the end of the war, I was about fourteen; he came into my room and just gave it to me. He told me to save it somewhere safe and someday when I fell in love, to give it to my forever husband." She paused for effect, murmuring, "You are my forever husband, Finn."

"I'm honored, darlin'," he whispered as he took his old watch out of his pocket, removed its plain standard chain, and attached her gift. Resettling the watch in its place, he leaned forward to take her lips with his for a kiss to seal the deal and, as always, their passion burned away the minutes, giving and taking, until they were both quite bothered and breathless.

Finally, she pushed him back and looked him straight in the eye. "But, just to set the record straight, Mister Maynard," she declared with a touch of sass, "I've considered myself your wife from the moment that judge back in Louisville declared it to be so, and I haven't wavered one bit...even that one time that I was so mad at you I wanted to knock some sense into your head," she laughed.

He threw back his head and joined in her joy. "Remind me never to make you mad again!"

She cocked her head and raised one eyebrow. "See that you don't, mister!"

CHAPTER 9

"Nervous, brother?" Sam snickered as he leaned close.

"Nah. Not nervous. Eager would be a better word," Finn corrected as he stood with his brother at the front of the church, his eyes trained on the double doors at the back, waiting for his bride to begin her walk down the aisle toward him.

What's she doing? It shouldn't take this long to make herself beautiful—she'd look gorgeous in a flour sack. His eyes slid closed and her image floated behind his closed eyelids...her waist length silky dark hair gathered over one shoulder as she brushed and braided it, her eyes glittering with mischievous joy as she shot back a teasing comment in response to one of his... *Come on, darlin', I wanna get this show on the road,* he silently fumed as he fidgeted in his borrowed black suit and reached up to tug at his new paisley cravat, which Sam had helped him tie—too tightly.

Reaching in his vest pocket, for the tenth time in the last

fifteen minutes, he removed his watch to ascertain the time. Slipping it back in, he perused the ship's wheel fob again. He'd been proud to tell his brother the story of it and how his bride had presented it to him.

Sam had been properly impressed.

To pass the time, he allowed visions of their two weeks of courting to drift past in his mind. The many excursions they had enjoyed together, such as the long walks along the river holding hands. Finn had been surprised at just how weakened his leg muscles were after his cast had been removed, but he worked hard, exercising it to restore strength to the limb and get it back to normal. The long walks had helped with that.

Several pleasant evenings were spent together enjoying the food at Brownville's different eateries. They had attended church twice as a couple and enjoyed buggy rides out into the countryside. Once, he even had the opportunity to impress his bride and play the hero when a rattler spooked their horse and caused him to take off in a wild gallop, while Finn yelled to Charise to hold on. He had valiantly brought the horse to a stop by sheer upper body strength and his bride had cooed and exclaimed about his muscles and bravery until he felt like he could conquer a nation. Plus, she had recounted the story to any who would listen. It was certainly an event to remember. He smiled now at the thought.

There were a few evenings when they had just strolled along the boardwalk arm in arm, nodding to everyone they passed and relishing the pure joy of having found one another. One evening, a glittering riverboat had docked boasting gambling, music, and dancing, and they had enjoyed a delightful, fun-filled night with many of the town's people who had boarded for a summer dance. Charise had been the belle of the ball in a gorgeous red dress she'd borrowed from Dottie, and Finn had been able to impress his new wife once again—this time with his dancing prowess as they had waltzed the night away—although he had regretted it the next morning when his newly healed leg had throbbed and complained from overexertion. *Oh well, it had been more than worth it.*

The following evening, Finn had sent an ever-helpful Toby to bring back a meal from the Blue Bird—fried chicken, mashed potatoes and greens, along with two servings of delicious peach cobbler—and he had set the table with his ma's best dishes, finishing it off with candles and flowers in the center. When Charise had come home from visiting Rachael, she had been splendidly pleased at the surprise and they had enjoyed a candlelit dinner together, alone. Oh, she had looked so lovely with those chocolate brown eyes of hers sparkling in the candle's glow. They had giggled and laughed, feeding one another bite after bite...sharing kiss after kiss after kiss...

That thought made him remember each night at day's end, when they would say goodnight at the door of their bedroom, kissing so passionately that Finn had to force himself to release his bride so that he could retire alone to the parlor to attempt another night's sleep on the settee. He was sure no other husband had ever volunteered to drive himself insane in such a way. Charise didn't know how many cold baths Finn had taken downstairs during the long nights, in an effort to survive the self-imposed fast. He shook his head at the thought. But, he had been determined to stay the course and keep his word that his bride would have a courtship to tell their children and grandchildren about, so help him!

Charise had spent her days making plans for the celebration after the nuptials with her new friends Rachael, Dottie, and even Elvira, and had worked to make sure her dress and veil were in top shape. She even helped Dottie make a new dress to wear when she stood up with Charise as matron of honor for their solemnization.

Finally, their second wedding day arrived and in keeping with the tradition of the groom not seeing the bride the morning of the wedding, Dottie and Dave had insisted Charise come and spend the night in the spare bedroom of their house next door to the jail. Thusly, Finn hadn't seen his wife in over twelve hours.

Twelve hours too long.

To say he was anxious and looking forward to the finality of their union would be the understatement of the century.

Sam's voice brought him back to the present as his brother gave a nod, hooking his thumbs in his suspenders and rocking back on his heels a bit. "You've got you one heck of a woman, Finny boy. I hope you know that. And you better treat her right or you'll answer to me."

Finn shot his brother a glare, but seeing the teasing glint in his eyes, he answered without malice. "You bet your life I know it. And I intend to spoil her and love her and cherish her for the rest of our lives, don't you worry."

Looking out at the people filling the pews of the church to help them celebrate their big day—so many people that were his friends and he'd known almost all his life—Finn saw several couples he knew to be happily married. He sent his brother a sideways glance.

"You know—turns out this mail-order-bride thing works pretty well. Take it from me, having a wife is much better than *batching* it. You ought to think about sending for one. That is...unless you've got your eye one someone here in town. *Elvira*, perhaps?" he added with a rude snort.

Sam turned appalled eyes his way, but before he could answer, the pianist—Elvira by coincidence—began to play the wedding march and everyone in the church stood to welcome the bride.

Dottie stepped back and regarded her handiwork. She and Rachael had been working on corralling Charise's long, sleek hair into a tight braided bun, with delicate, curling tendrils hanging down on either side. It had been slow going.

"I told you my hair is like silk and has a mind of its own," Charise commented as she turned this way and that, admiring the lovely chignon. "Believe me, by halfway through the party, it will slither its way out of most of its braid. It's so frustrating!"

Rachael laughed and gave Charise's back an affectionate pat. "Well, I'm sure it will hold at least during the exchanging of the vows. Your veil will help keep it in place. It's magnificent, by the way," she added as she and Dottie admired the lovely creation Charise had made by hand—Brussels type lace that depicted flowers, scrolls, and leaves. The ladies now affixed it atop her chignon with a Juliet cap and plenty of hairpins. Charise murmured her thanks for the compliment.

"The dress you made for Dottie is wonderful," Rachael complimented. "And *your* dress, Charise, is just beautiful. You are a superb seamstress. Have you thought of opening your own shop here in town?"

Charise met her friend's eyes in the mirror. "No, but...that's an idea. Perhaps in the unused space behind

Finn's shop area..." she mused, picturing just such a set up and wondering what Finn would think of it.

"Heaven knows the ladies of Brownville could certainly use another place to purchase clothing besides the cheaply manufactured garments Sebastian Hodge sells in his store." Then placing her hand over her mouth, the reverend's wife looked up to heaven and murmured, "Oh, Lord, forgive me. I meant no disrespect to Mr. Hodge. He's a fine man. He just...well, Lord, You know the man simply does *not* have good taste in women's fashion!"

Dottie and Charise both chuckled, however, because Rachael's description was accurate—about the clothing at the mercantile as well as Charise's wedding dress, which was a pure white silk sleeveless gown with a six-foot train and sheer voile overlay for the sleeves and across the bodice. A light green and ivory Victorian lady cameo necklace hung over the rounded neckline.

"Charise, your cameo is simply divine. I've never seen one with ivory on green like this," Dottie complimented as she picked up the pendent and examined the exquisite workmanship.

"Thank you," Charise murmured with a soft smile, gently taking it from Dottie's fingers and caressing the carved sculpture with her thumb. "It's the only piece of my mother's jewelry I was allowed to keep when everything was sold to pay my father's debts...Mama's favorite color was green and she had many dresses and blouses in various shades. Papa had given her this cameo on her last birthday before the war..."

The ladies both turned sympathetic eyes to the bride, but she merely shrugged with another smile. "It's all right. It was a long time ago...another life, really. Believe me, I'm much happier now than I've been since I was a small child."

Rachael took a big breath and glanced around the room, clasping her hands together. "Well, I think that does it. Do you have your old, new, borrowed and blue?"

The melancholy moment passed and Charise smiled at her two ladies in waiting. "Almost. For the borrowed, my friend Beth Ann sent me her best bracelet and earbobs, see?" she said as she reached for the objects she had laid on Dottie's vanity table earlier. The ladies *ooo'd* and *ahhh'd* as she slipped the pearls and gold jewelry on.

Rachael then reached for her own grandmother's lace hanky she had leant to her younger friend earlier and slipped it into Charise's hand. "This takes care of the old..."

"For the new, I purchased new undergarments at the mercantile," Charise reminded the ladies. "The only thing I'm missing is the blue," she added with a small lift of one shoulder.

As if on cue, there was a quiet knock at the door and

Dottie crossed over to open it. On the threshold stood a blushing Toby, only his eyes and the unruly mop of carrot red hair visible above an overly large bunch of flowers in his hands.

"M...Miz Maynard?" he stammered, shifting his gaze to see Charise as she rose from the vanity table stool. "Finn sent me out this mornin' to find you as many blue flowers as I could and said to bring 'em to you lickety split, so's you could have your *blue*...I'm not sure what that means. But I found you these—I hope they're all right...sorry it took me so long to get 'em to you..."

Charise's eyes moistened at that. She had only mentioned in passing that she hadn't found something blue to carry for the tradition, and Finn had taken care of it. *What a thoughtful husband he is!* She crossed the room to give the lad a kiss on the cheek as Dottie reached out and took the bunch from him, saying, "Thank you, Toby. They're amazingly lovely—and you got them here right on time, young man."

All three ladies delighted in the magnificently vivid spiderworts, prairie asters, and blue flax he had found as they sent him on his way with their sincere appreciation. Rachael and Dottie chuckled together and teased Charise about the young man's overzealous admiration toward her as they arranged them into a bouquet, tied with a bit of lace.

When finished, they placed it in Charise's hands and then fussed with the gown and train.

"Well...I guess I'm as ready as I can be," Charise announced and the ladies agreed. They ushered her out of the room and helped hold up the bottom of her dress as she climbed into the carriage Finn had rented for the day, with Dottie's husband, the sheriff—his star badge polished to a gleaming sheen—as the volunteer driver. Rachael joked that she hoped there were no hold ups or robberies while he was otherwise occupied.

Once they reached the church, Sebastian Hodge was waiting outside to walk her down the aisle. Over the weeks since her arrival, she had talked with the shopkeeper nearly every day and they had developed a fond relationship. So it was no surprise that he had readily agreed when Charise had asked him to walk her down the aisle for her and Finn's second wedding ceremony.

Now, the moment had come and they could hear music playing within. Her heart rate sped up and her scalp behind the tightly braided bun began to tingle.

"I don't know why I'm nervous—I'm only remarrying my husband," Charise joked. Nevertheless, she couldn't stop quivering.

"It's just wedding-day jitters. They'll pass once you get down the aisle and Finn takes your hand in his," Rachael assured her. Then the older woman leaned to give Charise an affectionate kiss on the cheek and whispered, "Just relax and take everything in. Make memories today. Bask in the love glowing in your groom's eyes." Then, she disappeared through the double doors on the sheriff's arm and took their places near the front.

Dottie and Charise exchanged grins and a quick hug as one of the ladies of the church opened the double swinging doors and propped them back. Then Dottie started down the aisle. Charise sent a trembling smile up at her escort and he smilingly winked and kindly gave her hand on his arm a reassuring squeeze as he moved them forward.

When Charise looked toward the front, just as Dottie arrived and stepped to the side, her eyes encountered those of her husband. Even from the back of the church, she could discern the sparkles in those beloved sapphire irises and those now familiar husband-induced tingles raced throughout her body.

The rest of the room seemed to fade away as she glided down the aisle to him...her darling Finn.

Charise knew she would cherish every memory of their vow-exchange for the rest of her life...Finn taking her hand in his and drawing her to stand beside him with their sides touching at the altar...Reverend McKnight's tranquil voice as he delivered a short message on the blessings of living in holy matrimony with God in the midst of a devoted relationship...the warmth of Finn's body at her side as he occasionally squeezed her hand.

And then, they turned toward one another to repeat their vows. This solemnization was different in every way from the first one; there was truly no comparison. Charise couldn't have taken her eyes from her husband's if she'd wanted to—and she didn't—as he earnestly promised to love, cherish, and keep himself only unto her *as long as they both shall live*. As he repeated the phrases, Charise's breath caught when tears of raw emotion gathered in his eyes. Hers immediately responded and it was all she could do to choke down her own emotions and speak forth her promises to love, honor, obey, and keep him in sickness and health. Rachael's grandmother's hanky was put to use.

Handkerchiefs were also discreetly used throughout the sanctuary as the guests witnessed the depth of adoration between the couple. Perhaps to provide a bit of relief from the seriousness of the moment, the reverend chose to joke that Charise had already shown she would tend to Finn's injuries, as she had met him when he had been at his worst. The gathered witnesses chuckled, as did the bride and groom.

Then Finn was slipping an ornate wedding band onto her hand and the reverend was pronouncing them husband and wife.

"Finn...you may now kiss your bride—and we all know you've had a quite bit of rehearsal at that," Reverend McKnight quipped, as indeed, everyone in town had seen the couple kissing at least once. Finn, never one to back down from a tossed gauntlet, scooped his wife into his arms, dipped her so low she gave a tiny squeal but held on, and gave her a wedding kiss the whole town was sure to remember. The entire church erupted in hoots, hollers and laughter.

When he finished, everyone had no doubt Charise had been well and thoroughly kissed.

Laughing and knowing her face must be the hue of a ripe tomato, she knew she had never been so blissfully embarrassed in all her life.

Then, her husband turned and announced to the guests, "All right, now we are well and truly married! Everyone is invited to come celebrate with us over at my shop. And no, it's not a tavern any longer, so don't be expectin' to get a beer with a chaser," he added with a grin, eliciting another round of chuckles and guffaws, and a few teasing shouts of disappointment.

At that point, it seemed everyone rushed forward to congratulate the happy couple and vie for hugs and kisses with the lovely bride—starting with Sam, the proxy.

"Well, don't you know that the Sharpes' ordered that there fancy, highfalutin' porcelain-lined cast iron bathtub all the way from Chicago? It took three months to get here. By the time it did, that there crate was so banged up, chipped up, and beat up, why we were all convinced that whatever was inside must surely be thrashed to a pulp. Fellas took bets on how much—or how little—of the porcelain was left in one piece! Why, that crate looked like it'd been through a war or somethin'! Old Bill Sharpe was almost afraid to pry the top off and look inside!" declared old Cyrus Ames as he regaled Charise and those nearby with the story of the traveling porcelain tub. "Yessiree, he was sure he'd done wasted his hard earned money, and he was cussin' a blue streak about wantin' his money back."

Finn snickered, watching his bride as she stood there in rapt attention, hanging onto every word the old man was saying—and the old coot was milking it for all he was worth.

"And?" Charise prompted, causing a few around them to chuckle. Everyone in the room knew the story but his wife.

"*And*," Cyrus stuck his hands deep in his trouser pockets and gave an exaggerated nod. "When he finally got up the nerve, steelin' himself for what he was about to see, and claw-hammered up the wooden topper, he saw that the crate was lined with material, like a flour sack, and inside it was full to the brim of what looked like real fine sawdust. He dug down in there and found the edge of the tub with his fingers and gave us all a glare, as we were ribbin' him somethin' awful. But he'd been determined he was gonna have the finest hotel and bathhouse in the whole of Nebraska. Well, a couple of us helped him tip it over, carefully, mind you, and when all the sawdust fell away—don't you know that there was not one scratch, not one chip, not one mark *anywhere* on that whole bathtub? *Except...*" He paused for effect, and gave her a wide half-toothless grin before tittering humorously, then said, "Except for one pinky toe was broke off of one claw foot. Ain't that the goll darndest thing you ever did hear?" he finished with a loud guffaw.

Everyone joined in the laughter and someone offered, "And it shore didn't take old Sharpe long to recoup his money. Heck, *everybody* wanted to come and take a bath in the famous travelin' porcelain tub!" That garnered another round of guffaws and laughs.

Finally, the guests that had gathered for the retelling of the story jovially shook their heads and then began to wander away.

Finn poured some refreshment for his wife and turned toward her as she giggled with one of the ladies.

"Another glass of cider for my beautiful bride?" he asked as he held a glass out to her—one of the glasses that had been stored under the bar and repurposed for the event.

Charise flashed him a bone-melting smile and took it from him with a breathless, "Thank you my handsome husband." The soft, breezy tone of her voice coupled with the look in her eyes made him almost swoop her up in his arms and run off upstairs with her, but he held himself still. *Easy there, Finn ol' boy. Just a little while longer. Breathe. Breathe.*

Settling for a risqué wink that promised mysterious pleasures in the near future, he resolutely turned as he sipped his own drink, allowing his gaze to roam the long room and the friends who were having a glorious time helping to celebrate their nuptials.

The downstairs had been transformed; they had spent days preparing, cleaning, scrubbing and arranging. The floor practically shined, his barber paraphernalia had all been compacted and pushed back to the front corner and covered with a flowered material, and all of the old tavern's tables and chairs had been brought back out, cleaned and arranged, covered in white tablecloths, and decorated with pretty ceramic oil lamps and borrowed china. There was not a spittoon, ashtray, or deck of cards in sight. The bar looked superb, having been artfully decorated with wedding decorations like ribbons and flowers. One end of the counter had been reserved for gifts and Charise had exclaimed multiple times over how many had been stacked there as the guests arrived.

Once they had cut the wedding cake and various attendees had offered toasts—via aforementioned glasses of cider—the party had gotten underway with song after song played by several of the townsmen who could play any kind of instrument. There was a banjo, a harmonica, a lively used set of spoons, a fiddle, and even old Mordecai Ellwood and his *singing saw*—an old hand saw and bow. With a grin as he watched him play, Finn thought, *the old geezer is in fine form today.*

Dottie and Dave danced by and Charise wiggled her fingers at them, prompting Finn to lean over and ask, "You rested enough, hon? I wanna get my lovely bride back out there on the floor for some more dancing and make all of Brownville's bachelors jealous."

She giggled and turned to place her half empty cup on the bar before taking his extended hand, and soon they were waltzing to a fair rendition of *The Blue Danube*. The band gamely followed that up with *My Old Kentucky Home*, in honor of the bride.

Charise glowed with happiness as he waltzed her around the floor. He couldn't take his eyes off her, this amazing woman who—for some unknown reason that he couldn't fathom but knew he would be amazed about for the rest of his life—had consented to leave her home to travel six hundred miles to be his wife. *How did I get so lucky? Well, in this case, second time's charm,* he mused, thinking of the mail order "bride" named Irma that had taken his money on false pretenses.

Holding his wife's gaze as they waltzed in perfect rhythm, he murmured, "Happy, darlin'?"

She blessed him with one of those special smiles she reserved for him alone. "Oh yes, Finn. I never *dreamed* I could be this happy. Deciding to marry you was the best decision I ever made," she added with a decisive nod.

"Oh honey, you don't know how glad I am that you *did*!" he answered, swinging her around one last time as the song came to an end.

She stretched up to place a warm kiss on his lips, and then whirled around to face the musicians. "Thank you for that wonderfully well-played reminder of home—well, of what *used* to be my home. Brownville is my home now." Turning in a circle, she met the eyes of those around her who were smiling in acceptance. "What a wonderful, peaceful town this is. I couldn't ask for more. Thank you all for welcoming me so joyfully."

Everyone murmured their approval before taking up their partners again as the musicians began playing, *Let me Call you Sweetheart.*

Dottie and Dave walked over, and Dottie gave Charise a

hug.

Just then, the bell atop the entry jingled as the door opened, and Finn glanced over to see Charlie, the telegraph operator, step in and look around the room. When he spotted Finn, he lifted a hand containing one of the telltale small, tan telegraph papers and waved it at him as he headed their way.

"Hmm, looks like Charlie's got a wire for me," he murmured to his wife as he released his hold on her and turned to greet the late arrival.

"Hey Finn. Sorry I'm late to your shindig. There was...a lot going on at the depot..." the man explained as Finn took the paper and read it quickly.

Smiling in amazement, he met Charise's questioning gaze. "I can't believe it."

Sam walked over to join the conversation, looking over Finn's shoulder at the paper. "Believe what, brother?"

Finn found his brother's eyes. "Would you believe, that woman, Irma, just wired me the money she owed me. I don't mind telling you, I thought there was no chance of *ever* seeing that money again. I'd chalked it up to an expensive lesson learned."

"Wonders never cease," Sam agreed.

Dottie and Charise exchanged glances as Dottie murmured, "I'm glad she made it right. That was terrible of her, what she did to Finn." Charise nodded in agreement and leaned close to clasp his arm against her side in a warm show of support.

Finn made to turn and take his bride in his arms again to join the dance, but Charlie cleared his throat. "Um...there's something else. Something that just came in on the train and I think is headed this way..."

Five pairs of eyes turned to him as Finn asked. "What's that, Charlie?"

The man took a breath to answer just as the front door opened again, the little bell over it jangling a merry warning, and a man stepped inside. Heads turned, the music came to a halt of sour notes and the dancers swirled to a stop as his presence was felt in waves of recognition. All talking and laughter ceased. Dishes and glassware waxed quiet as everyone in the room gaped and no one moved a muscle.

Finn couldn't believe his eyes as he recognized the newcomer looking around the room with a cool stare as if he had expected something different than what he was seeing. He wore a fine fitting gray suit with a wide string tie, his brown hair was combed smooth, and his chin whiskers were neatly clipped and short. The familiar, low-slung gun belt holstering a pair of matching pistols circled his hips, tied down in the way of a gunslinger. The uninvited guest unbuttoned his jacket and placed his hands on his hips just above the handles of the pistols as he addressed the room in general.

"What the he—" he paused for a split second as if choosing to acknowledge there were ladies in the room, "*Sam Hill* is goin' on here?"

Jumpin' Jehoshaphat, what's gonna happen now? Making this man angry is not healthy, and not something I particularly want to do...not with all these women present...and not on my weddin' night, for Pete's sake!

Keeping his gaze glued to the newcomer, his mind spinning with various scenarios and ideas, Finn felt his bride move and out of the corner of his eye, saw her lean closer to Dottie and whisper, "Who *is* that man?"

He heard Dottie mumble in reply, "My cousin Jesse. Jesse James."

CHAPTER 10

*C*harise couldn't take her eyes off the stranger and her heart leaped into a furious rhythm at her friend's words. *Jesse James?* **The** *Jesse James? Good heavens...does he intend to rob us? Will he shoot us? Surely he wouldn't with a member of his own family here...*

She cut her eyes toward her friend and swallowed hard, her heart thumping, as she observed that Dottie seemed to be a bit nervous herself as she watched the imposing figure in the doorway.

Charise then sought out her husband's profile, but he didn't meet her questioning eyes. He kept his face set and the clamped muscle in his jaw was the only indication that he was carefully not letting his thoughts or emotions show. He merely stared at the newcomer, as if waiting to see what the man...the *outlaw*...would do.

Jesse James allowed his hawkish gaze to sweep the room and to Charise's distress, he settled on *her*. Nervously, she swallowed again as he lowered his hands and slowly advanced with a loping, bow legged gait; all the while, the crowd was parting as if he were a cowcatcher on a locomotive, until he was standing directly in front of *her*. Unwittingly, his cold stare held hers and her head tilted back to maintain eye contact, as he was quite tall. That close, Charise saw that his irises were soul piercing, ice crystal blue, and they made her shiver all over as gooseflesh rose on her skin. Although his attention was focused on her, somehow, he gave the unnerving impression that he was aware of every person in the room, *and* what they were doing.

Finally, he allowed his eyes to sweep down her face and the rest of her body. As he stood there appraising her, Charise also took in his features, noting an oval face, a slightly pug nose, high cheekbones, dark sandy whiskers, and a very pale complexion. He wasn't ugly, she surmised, but then, he wasn't classically handsome like Finn, or ruggedly handsome like Sam. His face, however, was definitely what one might call...*memorable.*

Suddenly, he smiled as if he liked what he saw and held out a hand to her. Her eyes widened in shock as he grasped her left hand in his and she realized his were encased in leather gloves.

"I gather this is a weddin' party, and you are the bride," he commented, his voice deep and smooth. It didn't seem to bother him in the least that every eye in the room was watching his every move. It was almost as if he enjoyed the attention, basked in it...felt it was his due. The thought went through her mind that he enjoyed his celebrity status a tad too much.

Before Charise could gather her wits and answer, she felt Finn edge closer and slip a possessive arm around her shoulders as he spoke up, "That's right, James. This is our weddin' party, and this is my wife."

Then, the unfathomable outlaw sliced his ice edged focus toward Finn, and gave an ever-so-slight nod of acknowledgement, apparently not a whit surprised that Finn knew who he was.

"You're Maynard. Right? Phineas Maynard. You got a brother named Sam. You both served in the infantry under Thayer and Grant. First Regiment Nebraska Volunteers...*Yankees*," he sneered, giving Charise another shiver to think that a violent outlaw knew her husband's and brother-in-law's names and even knew the details of their service during the war. She couldn't know that the bandit made it a point to know particulars like that about the residents of the towns he frequented. Plus, since his cousin was married to the sheriff, he knew even more about Brownville's township.

"That's *right*," Sam and Finn replied in unison as Sam took a step closer, to stand shoulder to shoulder with his brother.

Suddenly, the imposing man let go of Charise's hand and turned fully toward the brothers, his gloved hands instantly moving to waist level at the ready—in what could only be interpreted as an aggressive move. The onlookers nearby gasped and Charise fought the urge to squeal in fright as everyone made to move back in heightened alarm. Finn put out a hand and firmly moved his wife behind his body.

"Hold on now, James. No need for that," Sheriff Dave snapped, steadfast as he moved to place himself at an angle between the outlaw and the brothers.

For Heaven's sake, what is happening? Charise released a silent scream as she grasped the back of her husband's jacket and peeked around the edge of his upper sleeve. She had just declared that Brownville was a peaceful little town, and now this? Would there be gunplay at her wedding reception? Then the thought hit home that Jesse James, a staunch Southerner who had fought ruthlessly as a Confederate soldier, probably still felt uncomfortable, angry, or even a bit threatened by *Yankees* although it had been ten years since the war ended.

Dottie quickly spoke up, "It's...it's good to see you, Jesse. How's your mother? And...and your wife, Zee? And how's Frank?"

James, his eyes narrow and watchful, flickered as he

looked at his cousin and gave a slow nod as if recognizing her attempt at smoothing over the situation. Seconds ticked by as heartbeats all around the room thundered, sweat broke out on palms and foreheads, and breathing quickened. Then after what seemed like an eternity of staring down the three men who had declared a united front of defense, despite the fact that none of them were armed, James seemed to relax a bit, his hands lowered to his sides, and he turned his head toward Dottie as he moved a step back.

"They're fine, Dot. Just came from Frank's weddin' up in Omaha, matter of fact. Thought I'd stop off here and get me a drink in my favorite tavern in all of Nebraska and maybe spend the night." He left the rest unsaid as he met Finn's eyes in question.

For several seconds, Finn remained silent and still. Part of Charise's brain was extremely proud of her husband as he stood up to the notorious outlaw, which everyone knew had killed in cold blood in the past with less provocation—if the newspaper accounts were correct. Charise could feel the tension coiled in Finn's body from her position directly behind. Finally, he spoke up, "I bought the building six months ago, James. It's no longer a tavern and hotel. It's my barbershop and home now."

One of the outlaw's eyebrows arched and he murmured, "That *right*?"

Finn continued to stand, his rigid posture and wide stance the only indication of his unease. "That's right. You're, uh...you're welcome to join us, if you've a mind to. However...I can't offer you any liquor," he added politely.

James stared at him silently for a few beats as if he were gauging Finn's courage or strength, switched his gaze to Charise, and then to Finn again with a shrug of a shoulder. "No thanks. Wouldn't wanna... *intrude*."

Then, he looked into Charise's astonished expression once more and smiled in a friendly manner, all traces of animosity gone as if magically wiped away. "Sorry to interrupt your party, Mrs. Maynard." As he met Dottie's eyes for a fleeting second, Charise detected a slight motion of his head before he turned on his heel and strode to the door, exiting and shutting it with a firm pull, though not a slam as she had expected.

Once the door closed, everyone in the room seemed to let out the collective breath they'd been holding. All at once, phrases were bandied about as folks murmured amongst themselves. "Can you believe that?" "Those Maynard brothers stood right up to Jesse James himself!" "I never thought I'd see the day he'd come struttin' in like that. Ain't he bold?" "That man's icy blue stare could make a stone statue shake with fear!"

Finn turned and Charise went straight into his protective

embrace as she felt herself begin to quiver from delayed reaction. His arms tightened warmly around her back.

"You all right?" he murmured against her temple and she answered with a nod against the satin vest of his wedding suit. Her eyes were shut, but she felt him move an arm and assumed he indicated that everyone should carry on with the party. The music slowly began again as the guests commenced their activities, some speaking quietly among themselves, with a few slowly dancing.

After a time, Charise gathered herself and stood apart from Finn, offering him a grateful smile before noticing her friend's perplexed appearance.

"I'm so sorry about that..." Dottie began.

"Dottie...I can't believe you're kin to...well, to *him*..."

Dottie exchanged eye contact with her husband. "Well, we're distantly related, on my mother's side. I knew him when we were children back in Missouri when his mother married Dr. Samuel. I spent a lot of time with Jesse's younger sisters and brothers... To be honest, however, I've never felt at ease around Jesse. He does have a quick temper if he gets riled...and now knowing what he's done and..." she paused and gave a thoughtful shrug.

Charise digested all this. Then a thought occurred to her and she turned to Dave. "But...isn't he wanted by the law? I mean...he's an outlaw and he robs trains and banks...right?

So...why didn't you arrest him?"

That made Dave obviously ill at ease, but he straightened his string tie and stood to his full height as he answered, "It's true he's wanted—in Missouri, Iowa, and Minnesota. But, he's never committed a crime in Nebraska. He has lots of family in the state and...well..." he glanced around, lowering his voice. "We have an understanding that he'll cause no trouble here. I've told him that if he ever commits any kind of crime anywhere in the state, or if a US marshal happened to be here with extradition papers, I'll have to set our friendship and kinship aside and do my duty as a man of the law. He knows I mean it, too. Dang fool," he broke off with a muttered curse. "He's so brazen. Someday it'll get him killed."

The couple exchanged looks again and a silent message seemed to pass between them. Dottie turned to Charise, leaning near to give her another hug. "Congratulations on your wedding honey. It was wonderful. Everything turned out beautifully. But now I, um...I need to go and...see about...*him*," she finished, before straightening in much the same way her husband had just done, as if she were preparing herself for something unpleasant, and headed for the door. Dave put on his hat, tipped it at the newlyweds, and followed her out.

Just then, Cyrus ambled up to Finn and whacked him on the sleeve. "Well doggies, never saw the like. The famous outlaw Jesse James comes to town on your weddin' day and crashes your party. Don't know whether that's good luck or bad!" he cackled, scratching his head as if he were trying to figure it out. "But you can take it either way. I'd say think of it as you two ain't gonna have one dull day of married life!" He let out another cackle and wandered away to the refreshment table.

Charise and Finn looked at one another, and started to laugh. Once again, the old coot had managed to cut through the bull and address the horns.

Several hours later, the tension from the unexpected visit the outlaw paid them had waned, the last of the wedding guests had finally left and Finn locked the front door. Charise was so relieved. Although the evening had been eventful, to say the least, the day had been drawn out and tiresome and she had yearned for it to be over so that she and Finn could find their new *normal*.

Now that the day was finished, however, Charise found herself unexpectedly nervous and shy, so she busied herself with picking up glasses and plates, deep in thought about actions that were still a bit of a mystery, but would be taking place quite soon. Would tonight go well? Would she...well...*please* her husband? By the same token...would he please *her?* And...what exactly did that entail? Oftpondered worries and concerns rose to the forefront of her mind and she wished she had asked for more details of her two married friends.

All of a sudden, a pair of very strong arms slipped around her from the back and she stilled with a soft smile and allowed Finn to draw her back against his chest.

Closing her eyes, her lips parted as she nestled against him and breathed in his scent—a pleasant mix that was uniquely Finn and a faint lingering of the bay rum he had splashed on after his morning bath and shave. She relished his warmth as he nuzzled her cheek with his smooth lips and murmured, "I can't believe we're finally alone—and married. And no more trying to sleep on that blasted settee," he added with a soft snicker as he nipped at the lobe of her ear, causing a delicious little shiver to shoot over her shoulder, down her arm and over her skin—all the way to the hidden recesses of her body. Finn's lips roamed the area behind her ear and his hands began a decidedly husband-like exploration of private areas he had not yet dared to touch.

Finally, Finn turned Charise in his arms and his lips covered hers as she opened to him for a passionate kiss. The plates she was holding slipped onto the table, but mercifully didn't break, as she couldn't help but slip her arms up and around his neck, kissing him back with equal fervor. Oh, how she loved this man!

With a suggestive growl, her husband swept her up in his arms, white silk voluminous skirts and all, and turned for the interior steps. She couldn't help but giggle at his impatience.

"Finn...put me down...I can walk...there's not room enough for both of us at once..." she tried to speak in between Finn's persistent kisses.

"I'll manage," he vowed as he ravished her mouth again before taking the steps two at a time, twisting her around as he went and having not one bit of trouble.

Another soft giggle escaped as they reached their bedroom door. "It appears your leg is completely healed now..."

He shoved the door open with his foot to prove the point, and noticing the flickering candlelight inside, she vaguely remembered that Dottie had hinted she would get the room ready for their special night. However, she didn't see the many candles, flowers, and the turned-down bed, for she had eyes and heart only for Finn as he murmured against her lips, "Yes ma'am, and I'm about to show you just how healed and whole your husband *is*."

"Finn!" she gasped, at once feeling both thrilled and embarrassed by his frank declaration.

He chuckled as he gently set her down on the edge of the bed and went down on one knee, capturing her lips again with electrifying passion.

Tenderly, he began the removal of her wedding finery and, feeling emboldened, she helped him with his and then, with smiles of true bliss, they blew out the bedside candles together.

Their wedding night had finally arrived.

Charise climbed the steps to her home, as always admiring the fine craftsmanship of the new staircase as she grasped the handrails, and having finished hanging a load of laundry on the line, poured herself a cup of coffee from the pot on the kitchen stove. She strolled contentedly down the hall to the front room, sipping the hot brew, and stood gazing out the window at her neighbors and friends going about their business on the street below. After a few minutes, she settled at her desk by the window.

Taking up paper and pen to write her friend, she paused to collect her thoughts before starting...

Dearest Beth,

I've been a true wife for a week now, and I've never felt so completely happy, fulfilled, and content in my life. I'm so in love with my husband—and he with me. It's truly an answer to many prayers and a dream come true! His leg has fully healed and he is back to normal—and I'm pleased to tell you he is quite romantic and virile. After only a week of marriage, I no longer blush to write such things. Are you shocked? I'm chuckling as I put pen to paper and wish I could see your face as you read.

Oh Beth, our wedding was beautiful—I wish you could have been here, but thank you so much for the use of your bracelet and earbobs. They are carefully enclosed.

Charise paused a moment, contemplating, before filling her friend in on more particulars of the wedding, and especially Finn's surprising her with her overly large, amazingly blue bouquet. Then with a giggle, she continued...

Now, I will tell you about our unexpected visitor. As our wedding reception was in full swing, with everyone waltzing, eating cake and having a wonderful time—and just after I'd said out loud to all my new friends and neighbors that I loved my new town of Brownville because it was such a quiet, peaceful place—the door opened and a man came in. Dear friend, it was none other than the outlaw, Jesse James! No, I'm not making that up.

He came in because our building used to be, in his words, his favorite tavern in all of Nebraska! He'd visited there many times in the past and even stayed in the hotel! He hadn't heard that the tavern was no longer in operation, so he stalked in and made a show of being fierce in his disappointment of the saloon being closed, until my husband, Sam, and our sheriff, stood up to him. My heavens, he even let Finn know that he knew his name and where he served during the war! It was far beyond nerve-wracking. If I were the type of woman who succumbed to the vapors, it would have been a perfect time. For a few seconds, I wondered if my wedding day would end with me becoming a widow! Especially when Finn shoved me behind him, with the intent of using himself as a shield if bullets started flying.

But then, the interloper backed down and actually apologized for intruding. Gracious me, Jesse James is without a doubt the most intimidating man I've ever met in my life—and I hope to never encounter him again!

You see Dottie is actually a distant cousin to the outlaw, by marriage I think. We found out later that he made his unexpected visit to town because a friend of his apparently convinced him to pose for a daguerreotype portrait at a studio in Nebraska City! Can you believe that, the audacity! Jesse James, with a price on his head—dead or alive no less—doesn't care who knows what he looks like. He rides trains in Nebraska and saunters down the streets, stays in the finest hotels, enjoys drinks in taverns, and visits family, apparently without fear of reprisal. The fact that he's never committed a crime in Nebraska seems to make all the difference. If I hadn't experienced it myself, I'd never believe it.

I saw a copy of the portrait, by the way—he gave a miniature of it to Dottie—but it does not do him justice. By that I mean it doesn't show the potent intimidation his mere presence in a room engenders. His eyes are a cold ice blue. Remembering them still makes me shudder. I had no problem believing he could shoot a man dead and not bat an eye.

It seems that the bandit recently married another cousin of his named Zerelda, and his brother, Frank also recently wed. Isn't that amazing in itself? What kind of woman would marry a known outlaw? Dottie says he told her he's been looking at buying some land in Franklin, Nebraska, and that he and Frank want to settle down and live "respectable" lives, have children, and the whole nine yards—after, that is, one more heist to get the money to finance it! Heaven's to Betsy. I didn't say it to her, but I feel that Mr. James will come to a bad end. Papa used to say, those who live by the sword or the gun die by the sword or the gun.

Dottie told him she didn't want to know any details about what he or his gang may or may not be planning. She actually told him that as family she feels a spark of loyalty toward him, but as the wife of a sheriff, and a law-abiding citizen, she was torn. He told her he respected her truthfulness and would abide by her and her husband's wishes. So he stayed the night, after indulging in a few drinks at the Lucky Buck, and left on the train the next day.

The oldsters say it was the first time that the outlaw had visited the town in such a barefaced manner. Before, he had always laid low and few knew he had even been in town until after he had left. His lucky breaks seem to have gone to his head. Perhaps, he feels invincible.

Ah well, that's enough on that subject. Let me tell you the latest teasing caper that my two "husbands" fooled me with...

"Charise? Where are you, honey?" Finn called just then, interrupting her train of thought.

She smiled happily and carefully placed her pen aside as she called, "In the front room, sweetheart!"

His footsteps sounded in the hall and then he appeared at the doorway, a huge smile gracing his face.

At the sight of him, her heart gave a familiar little flip, as it always did. He was dressed in his normal everyday clothing, white shirt, dark blue vest and trousers. His watch chain hung in a loop from his vest pocket, and at the sight of it she smiled even brighter, remembering the night she presented him with the fob. When he was at work, he never wore a tie, but even so... *Ahh, Finn Maynard, what a handsome specimen you are. And you're all mine!*

"You'll never guess," he exclaimed as he stepped forward and grasped her hands to tug her from her seat and then wrapped her up in his arms. Leaning back, he planted a firm kiss to her lips and pulled back with a smack, chuckling at his mysterious news.

She laughed with him. "What, Finn? Good heavens, don't keep me in suspense!"

Her husband wiggled his eyebrows at her and grinned again. "I heard it from Charlie, and not my brother—but Sam went and did it."

Her brow furrowed. "Did what?"

"He sent a wire to one of those matrimonial agencies. Your *proxy husband*, my dear, just sent off to find a mail-order-bride for himself!"

Great day in the morning – the adventure continues!

THE END---for now

But coming in March of 2019 – A BRIDE FOR SAM

Author Notes

While doing preliminary research for this story and trying to decide just where my hero would live and my girl would have to travel to, I came across Brownville, Nebraska. Immediately, I fell in love with images of the quaint little town, which is still in existence. Many of the town's original buildings are still there and the history is well preserved. They have a website and it seems that it would be a wonderful place to check out on vacation. In my story, I used as much of their real history as I could. Here is their website: Welcome to the Merchants of Brownville

Next, I needed a location to use for my hero and his bride to live and was lucky enough to stumble upon a wonderfully informative Facebook page for The Lone Tree Saloon. Yes, it's a real place, still there, and much of my descriptions were true to its recorded history. I hope to be able to make a trip there sometime and see the building after the renovations are finished.

Now, one more thing... Did you wonder if I went off the deep end with my Jesse James appearance and connecting him to Brownville the way I did? Well, I didn't! In my research, I stumbled upon the fact that he frequented Brownville, that the sheriff, David Plasters was a friend of the outlaw's and was married to one of Jesse's cousins, *and* that the Lone Tree Saloon was his favorite watering hole, so I just couldn't resist including him in my story to add a bit of pizzazz. Check out this page: Jesse James in Nebraska

Happy Reading!

I hope you have enjoyed the fifth book in the brand-new series, The Proxy Brides. New books will be released every other week through 2019.

If you enjoyed this story, I would appreciate it if you would leave a review, as it helps me reach new readers and continue to write stories that appeal to you.

Leave a review here:

https://www.amazon.com/Linda-Ellen/e/B00QDAXSSW/

Acknowledgements

First of all to my Lord and Savior, Jesus Christ—You're always there for me!

Steve, my wonderful husband, number one cheerleader, biggest fan, and plot partner—I love you!

Venessa Vargas, Kathryn Lockwood, Judy Glenn and Liz Austin, my editor, proofer, and betas—Couldn't navigate this journey without you guys!

Friends in **Clean Indie Reads, Proxy Bride Authors**, and **Louisville's Past** Facebook groups—you guys rock!

And last but not least, to all of my loyal fans who are always excited when I put out another book—this one's for you!

Upcoming Proxy Bride Books (2018 Series)

A Bride for Jeremiah by Christine Sterling

A Bride for Clay by Marianne Spitzer

A Bride for Nathan by Barbara Goss

A Bride for Abel by Cyndi Raye

A Bride for Finn by Linda Ellen

A Bride for Carter by Wendy May Andrews

A Bride for Charles by H. L. Roberts

A Bride for Sterling by Parker J. Cole

A Bride for Henry by P. Creeden

Books are released every two weeks! Join my newsletter to make sure you see the 2019 publication schedule!

https://lindaellenbooks.weebly.com/contact.html

About the Author

Linda Ellen lives in Louisville, Kentucky with her husband of thirty-seven years. A lifelong avid reader, and after encouragement from her family and friends, she tried her hand at writing in 2009 and never looked back. Prior to the release of her debut novel *Once in a While* (fashioned from the real-life story of her parents' romance), she wrote articles for a local newspaper, *The Southwest Reporter*. Linda keeps very busy with her work in her church's prison ministry and writing every spare moment she gets. Many more plans are under way for books and series, both historical and modern day.

To keep up with the latest news on her books, including trailers, cover reveals, release dates, and book signings, visit and "like" her Facebook page, Linda Ellen – Author (see below for link) For a special treat, go to her Pinterest page to see many pictures related to all of her stories

Linda loves to hear from readers. You can contact her in any of these ways:

Email - LindaEllenBooks@gmail.com
Website - www.lindaellenbooks.weebly.com

VISIT ME ON SOCIAL MEDIA!

Twitter: @lindaellen54

Facebook - https://www.facebook.com/LindaEllen.Author/

Follow her on her Amazon Author Page to be alerted to her new releases!

OTHER WORKS BY LINDA ELLEN

AVAILABLE ON AMAZON, B&N & KOBO

THE CHERISHED MEMORIES SERIES
Book one – Once in a While
Book two – The Bold Venture
Book three – Almost as Much

SOLDIERS OF SWING SERIES
Her Blue-Eyed Sergeant
Her Blue-Eyed Corporal
Her Blue-Eyed Lieutenant

MAPLE HEIGHTS SERIES
Sweet Love at Honey Landing

If you enjoyed this book, please check out the <u>Christian Indie Author Readers Group</u> on Facebook. Opportunities abound to find other clean or Christian Authors and learn about new releases, sales, and free books. Another great Facebook group to join if you enjoy sweet western romances like this one is <u>Sweet Wild West Reads</u>, a wonderful place where sweet western romance authors and readers discuss their favorite stories, thoughts, and authors. Contests and giveaways happen weekly. Join the group today!

Another opportunity to find good, clean books to add to your collection is the <u>Clean Indie Reads</u> website. It's the home of Flinch Free Fiction of every genre. Check it out today!

And finally, take a look at the <u>Kentuckiana Authors</u> website, where there is "Too much talent for just one state. We are traditional, small press, and independent authors, and there is something for everyone!"

Made in United States
Orlando, FL
17 June 2024

Made in United States
Orlando, FL
17 June 2024